J.S. Scholz

Little Islands
and other stories

Acknowledgements

I can't thank Janet enough for her sustained support, love, encouragement, freshly caught fish and amazing culinary expertise.

Thanks beyond words also to my amazing daughters and extended family.

Thank you to my steadfast friends for always believing in me.

Many of these stories were written while I was a high school teacher. Thus, I thank my teaching colleagues from Grant High School in Mt Gambier, Streaky Bay Area School, Mount Compass Area School and the Australian Science and Mathematics School at Flinders University. Also, the students I taught (or rather, who taught me). Your resilience, courage, talent and kindness make me feel positive about the future of our world. Lead first with kindness.

The wonderful Sand Writers are a constant source of inspiration. In that little church meeting room on a Goolwa back street, I get to hear and read some of the most beautiful poetry and prose ever. Sand Writers, you are a gift to me and the world. Of that group, the following have had a great influence on me through their astounding writing, encouragement and wise counsel: Jude Aquilina, Julie Cahill, Keith MacNider, Roger Rees and Heather Webster. National treasures all. Thank you.

Lastly, thanks to the judges and organisers of writing competitions around Australia, along with publishers (like Ginninderra Press) with a bias for yes – keep it up. We need you.

First published 2018 by
GINNINDERRA PRESS
PO Box 3461 Port Adelaide 5015
www.ginninderrapress.com.au

Little Islands

Contents

The Poetry of Time

Car bodies shunt and clatter on the factory production line. Metal skeletons shuffling. The hot rivet-welding gun is brick-heavy in the new lad's hand. School, poetry, essays, exams – where his brain froze with the terror of expectation, the resulting disappointment – are a world away. A world now closed off by steel, time clocks, deafening noise.

Behind him, another car body squeaks and clunks into riveting range. He skips back, roof-suspended riveter cables writhing above. His one and only job is to weld rivets around the back window edging of each car with the heavy electric gun. Stretching towards the coming car body, he starts welding the rivets into the bare steel frame of the back window. Clonkfzz, clonkfzz, clonkfzz, clonkfzz, twenty-eight times around the window rim, evenly spaced hot little mushroom rivets and it's done. He looks at his watch. Thirty-five seconds. Pretty good.

His life has become a calculation of time and fusing metal. No more Gerard Manley Hopkins, no poetry, no books.

Bruno, a door hinger, walks past, looks at the job and flashes a crooked thumbs up. The old man shouts something above the din, Brylcreemed grey hair shining, round face beaming.

Each car body is in riveting range for one minute and fifty seconds. If the boy does one as soon as it's in range and the next two quickly, he earns just under one minute of freedom. Not enough. It takes twenty seconds to walk out of the factory and twenty to get back to his station on the production line. That leaves too few seconds to stand out in the sun, suck in the air, smell the shrubs and sugar gums confined in their little garden beds between the ribbed-steel factory wall and the traffic-snarled street.

Or do the crossword in *The Advertiser* hidden under the bench, read the paper in stolen moments and be restless as a caged tiger. If Mick, the leading hand, is doing his rounds, it takes a bit longer, but strangely seems faster. As if time speeds up when he has to keep an eye out for the leading hand. Or in ten seconds he can walk over to Bruno, have a few words, and run back to his riveter.

But it's the rectangle of light jutting into the metallic factory air that calls him. He longs to be able to stand out there and feel the sun, dream of the world spinning and be in it. Out there, he can close his eyes and remember the farm. Tall gum trees in the creek, parrots flashing blue red in the sun, kookaburras laughing at the morning.

Out there beside the steel wall of the factory, his ears can rest from the clangs and shouts, the heavy tread of Mick coming up behind, trying to catch him reading or daydreaming. Out there, he can look up at the sky and see the silver trails of jets, imagine where they're going, envying movement and space, a vast world he can only read and dream about.

The car bodies keep coming. The bosses are edgy. Yesterday someone threw a bolt on the line, jamming it for twenty minutes. Mick stalks the factory workers, hands on hips, eyes burning into overalled backs. Pete, the foreman, stalks him. Somewhere, behind soundproof glass, someone stalks Pete.

The rivets weld on the same way, though, car after car, hour after hour, day after day. Clonkfzz, clonkfzz, clonkfzz, twenty-eight rivets evenly spaced.

The crossword is coming without effort or challenge. Twelve down, five letters, sacrificial table? – Altar. Build, five letters? – Erect. Damn, too easy. Clonkfzz, clonkfzz, clonkfzz, twenty-eight times.

'What the hellerya doin', boy?' Mick's voice is a stab in the back.

'Nothing, just waiting for the next body. Everything's fine.'

'Well, stand at the line, not over here at the bench. I want to know you're concentratin' on the job. What's that?' His piercing eyes are arrowed down to the shelf space under the bench. The newspaper is hanging half out like a sail. 'Hey, there'll be none o' that either.' He reaches down, scrunches up the newspaper and thrusts it in the boy's face. A bony thumb is pressed into a footballer's face on the back page. 'If I ever see you readin' the paper on the job again, your feet won't touch the ground!'

'Sorry. But look at the riveting. It's good.'

'That's not the bloody point, dickhead, is it? You're not paid to read the bloody paper. You will stand right here and watch the line, even if you've got nothin' to do.'

Bruno is hinging the back door on a station wagon, but the boy can feel him watching. 'No worry, young one. All be right,' he'll say on the drive back to Woodville tonight, rubbing his stubby thighs.

The old bloke lives for his wife and children and grandchildren. Boyhood memories of a village in Campania. And the Company. He likes them – more than they like him since arthritis slowed his hands. Next week will be his retirement, time counted precisely by the company. Decades of hinges.

Clonkfzz, clonkfzz, clonkfzz, twenty-eight times, evenly spaced. The boy knows he won't be able to stand this without the little reading breaks earned by stretching that riveter cable down the line. Not without Bruno's company anyway.

That night, he goes through all his old books, scrabbling like a starving man, trying to find one small enough to hide easily in his overalls' pocket. *Heart of Darkness*. He remembers now. Boats, journeys, prisoners, rivers. Africa. It seems more powerful now than when he was at school and had to analyse it, write essays about it and other books. He knows a bit more about the world now, about being trapped, your soul withering inside you.

Bruno's going and it's a big thing in the factory. Everyone knows and likes him. The company loves loyalty. But not arthritis. On his last day, the boy drives the old man to work. Big crooked hands slide up and down the old thighs, rubbing rubbing, rhythmic as a clock. Bruno wears a grin as usual, but this day it doesn't reach to his brown eyes. *Heart of Darkness* is a flat rectangle in the boy's hip pocket. The weirdness coming from Bruno silences them in the sleepy morning. It is a morning like all the others – of asphalt and traffic lights, the acrid stink of a cacophony of endless exhausts, commuters blinking and yawning behind car windows.

In the factory, Mick is edgy, his face all hard lines and planes of tension, like a newly machine-pressed car bonnet. Even Pete comes out onto the floor, inspecting the work minutely. He looks out of place in his white shirt and darting eyes, recoiling at a smudge of grey metal grease that appears on his sleeve.

The boy feels himself going mad. The book stays pocketed, the car bodies shuffling obediently up to be riveted. Mick glares at him, appears and disappears without warning. Suddenly a line from Gerald Manley Hopkins pops into his head like a hot rivet – *all is seared with trade; bleared smeared with toil;* Funny, to remember all this poetry now and not during the exam. The lunch siren blasts five minutes early.

This is it, the farewell for Bruno. The ritual of the company acknowledging a life loyally given to steel, hinges, welding, paint. The men and women in this section of the line, sixteen overalls, gather around Bruno, who stands nervously next to neatly suited Pete. It's done quickly, the handshake, the gold watch, applause and back-slapping.

Bruno looks at the watch and reverently buckles it around his wrist. The Victoria Cross of the factory worker. 'Good watch, eh?' he says to the boy. 'Keeps good time too. You get one one day?'

Twenty-five years – he will be in his forties. That's ancient. Decades of riveting, five minutes extra for lunch and a gold watch. The better to count seconds. And in here, each second is a lifetime.

Some of the lads dash to the pub for quick beers – strictly forbidden, but hey, it's Bruno's last day. So what if he doesn't come? We'll have one for the old bugger.

In the precious half hour before the line restarts, Bruno and the boy move a laminated cafeteria table into the sun. Bruno has brought his wife's delicious pizza campofranca for their final factory lunch together.

Driving home, Bruno stares at the cracked windscreen, his palms shhing back and forth on his thighs. He's got his favourite fawn strides on, shiny and faded with rubbing. A tear slides down the old cheek, dodges his moving hands and splotches dark as blood on the palm polished fabric.

The next week on the floor, it's as though Bruno never was. Mick is almost smiling. A girl from dashboards, nimble-fingered and fast, puts hinges on in Bruno's spot. Also, they've automated another welder, taken a worker out. The car bodies come faster, relentless as an overwhelming army. A whole new arithmetic of time has to be worked out.

Pete is beaming. 'An extra body going through pre-paint every half hour!' he declares, stroking his tie, keeping well away from the grease of the line.

Clonkfzzz, clonkfzzz, clonkfzzz, twenty-eight rivets. How many seconds? Days? Weeks? Decades. A gold watch. Time.

Late in the long afternoon, with warm sun spilling sharply through that door, the boy pulls on the rivet gun's cables, trying to make them stretch. Maybe he could race down the line of back windows and add to his seconds of freedom. He pulls so hard one of the clips pings off the steel struts holding the cable above him. The cable groans, shimmies and flops an extra car-length down. He looks around quickly. No one sees.

Clonkfzzclonkfzzclonkfzz, he's going down the metal river of car bodies like a madman. Five rear windows before he runs out of cable. Perfect job too. No sign of Mick or Pete. Beauty. He puts the rivet gun on the steel bench, looks around, and heads for the door.

Soon he's outside sucking in the vivid afternoon air. Through the spindly sugar gums trapped between the factory and the street, a breeze smells of the gulf, of journeys yet to take. Curled exquisitely cylindrical, a dry leaf, a spider's penthouse, hangs trapezed from radiating webs. Skin hungry for sun, he rips open overall studs and peels off to the waist. Light bounces. Ahhh! *all this juice and all this joy, a strain of the earth's sweet being.* Hopkins again in his head. Only now does he truly understand what the poet meant. The boy closes his eyes, opens his arms and points his face to the blue sky.

The fist on the back of his head rocks him forward, stumbling into the sap streaked trunk of a tree. Spoggies shrapnel the air, cars hum on the street, a bus changes gear, coughing out diesel smoke.

Mick grabs a fistful of hair and wrenches the young face into his. *Heart of Darkness* spills to the ground and is stomped and minced with steel-capped boot. 'Listen, you little shit, think you're smart with your newspaper and wanker books?'

Hair starts to uproot, spit dances in the sunlit air.

'You get back on the line and if you move one inch from your station again, that'll be it. You'll be history like that bloody crippled old dago mate of yours!' He pushes the boy to the factory door.

Heart of Darkness bounces off the boy's stinging scalp. Strangely he doesn't feel humiliated, just propelled. He leans down, picks up the book, and strides through the clanging factory, past overalled bodies hunched over steel skeletons, past spot-welding stations with their crab arms and fizzing spark showers, towards the pay office.

Alarmed at such disobedience, Mick pursues him. 'Hey, dickhead, where you think you're goin'?'

The boy turns, pauses. The thing is, he doesn't know. Somewhere beyond counting time, far from where seconds have to be stolen, where the world does not pass by without him being in it. But no worry. All be right.

'To get some pizza!' he shouts back.

Shooting Clouds

Nanna is sitting up in her hospital bed, flicking through the pages of a *Women's Weekly*. Occasionally she shakes her grey head and stabs a finger at a page. If she doesn't like the hairdo, she shakes her head; if she likes a particular one, she purses her lips. Silver lines of saliva slide from her mouth corners, disappearing under her pale chin. But mostly there's just the steady swoosh of the glossy pages fanning her creased face.

The ward is full of old-people smells, washed in white light. A pink nurse squeaks past and my eyes follow her along the mesmerising lines of white and purple lino.

With her free hand, Nanna holds my arm tightly, a hostage in case Mum and Dad make a run for it. Dad is sitting in a hospital chair inspecting something under a fingernail, one foot tapping rhythmically in its scuffed boot.

A machine beeps somewhere. Mum eventually prises off Nanna's grip and gives Dad a nod. She talks softly to Nanna but the big tears start to fall and join up with the saliva. Dad puts his arm around Mum, steers her towards the door, and I turn to Nanna and whisper a promise.

'I'm saving my hair for you, Nanna.'

Dad sits high up on the open tractor. The big diesel clatters to idle as he closes the throttle lever with a smack of his palm. He steps down, towering over me in his army surplus jacket. His eyes are red-rimmed and leaking from the drifts that float up and shroud the moving tractor and its driver in an abrasive storm. 'Any news on Nanna?' he asks.

'Still the same. More tests or something.'

'Mm. Talking at all?'

'No.'

He climbs back onto the machine with the brick of sandwiches I've brought, punches the throttle and the great machine lumbers forward pluming diesel smoke. The seeder slices lines of wheat seed and super phosphate into the dry dirt. Blazing noise and dust, sprays of sand flying off the tyre lugs and into his face, he sails off on his dry sea of dirt and I run back to the warm island of the ute.

The next day at school, we're picking teams for a senior girls' netball game. Terri and Toni the athletic twins are the captains as usual. I stare at the cracks in the asphalt. Please don't pick me last. The twins haggle over the tall fast girls who want the ball more than anything. I don't care about the stupid ball at all, but I don't want to be picked last. Soon they're down to the last two, Chubs and me. My face stings. Chubs is slow but impossible to get round. I'm fast but I never get the ball. I try but I can't work up a desire to chase it. I love to run, but through scrub or down paddock tracks that promise distance and things to see, not in endless ricochets after a ball. Besides, my brain is still full of my father's sand blasted eyes, Nanna's finger stabbing at the glossy page.

'Chubs!' comes the call and I shuffle quickly off to the other team, intently looking for patterns in the asphalt.

'C'mon, Chicken Legs, just try not to stuff up this time.' Terri slaps me on the back, so hard it stings.

I stumble forward, trying not to hear the smirks rising in the air like sand off tractor tyres.

Next day, we're on one of our trips into town to see Nanna again. We round the bend just before the bitumen of the town begins and there she is, on the side of the dirt road shuffling along, bent over with her head down like one of those refugees on the telly. A wispy mirage in her flapping hospital gown and grey hair.

'Cripes!' Dad hits the skids.

Mum leaps from the car while it's still going.

Nanna looks up and starts waving and grinning like she's just come back from a holiday. They hug like long-lost sisters, and then Mum pops her in the back with me.

Nanna reaches out a hand, pulls me in, curling against her.

'Turn round. We're going home,' says Mum.

'Good idea.' Dad winks at us two skinny girls in the rear-vision mirror.

'Home,' says Nanna.

Mum turns round. It's the first word Nanna's said since the stroke.

Winter plods into spring school holidays and the wheat Dad has sown is struggling to stay alive on the few small rain showers we've had. But Nanna is home and she's all right. Smiling all day long, listening to her Nana Mouskouri records, going through piles and piles of magazines. Stopping her page turning only at David Beckham's spiky hairdo. Pursing her lips and tapping his head.

One warm Saturday, Nanna and me are left alone on the farm. Above us, the shed cackles and stretches in the September sun. Out in the paddocks, sparse lines of thirsty wheat stretch to scrub blotched horizon. The pink smear of the dam track looks like a broken rubber band through the crop. Nanna is smiling in the passenger seat of the ute, sharp face shaking and giggling, feet tapping.

'Better get going, before they get back.' My voice rattles with anxiety, neck swivelling, checking that Mum and Dad have really gone into town. The livid afternoon, the forbidden dam, are all ours.

Nanna giggles, all gums and spit. 'Going!' she says.

I crunch in a gear, the ute leaps forward, and we're out of the shed and passing under the sighing trees. We scoot along the track and over the hill to the dam. Nanna is singing, *And I love you so, people ask me how, how I live till now, I tell them I don't know...* Flowers in her voice float out over the paddock.

Soon the dam looms out of its familiar fringe of trees. A brown snub of water in a grove of remnant mallee. The water is low for this time of year but there's enough for a good swim.

Later, I'm stretched out under a tree on a slab of cool granite. Nanna is in her deckchair in a summer dress, covered in pale blue flowers. Around us is the debris of our celebration picnic filched from the kitchen – a tin of Milo and a fizzing big bottle of lemonade. My mouth is syrupy. A flock of galahs squeal and feint at the water before settling on the other side. Oh, the delicious mischief of it. The stern voice of Mum telling us about the boy who drowned here in the fifties, the perilous icy pull of the still water just below the warm surface. 'Never ever swim in a dam. You'll get cramp. Kids drown in dams!' And to me the expectation that I will look after Nanna, take her for a walk. Ha! She looks after me.

'Wish it would rain.' I swivel my head to her, feeling the wet scratch of granite on the back of my skull.

'Rain,' Nanna instructs the cloudless sky.

That night, we're watching the telly, Dad stretched out on the vinyl recliner, Nanna on the couch, mouth open, eyes closed, me next to her. News of the drought blasts from the screen. The long El Niño, they call it. A bloke from the CSIRO is talking about cloud seeding. The recliner squeaks and I can feel Dad's brain ticking over. The weather map shows a promising low pressure heading right for us.

'If we get some rain from this system, we can still get a good crop,' he says. 'That cloud seeding could work here, I reckon. Just put something in the clouds for the water droplets to form around?' he asks the CSIRO bloke who has gone real quiet, staring up at the sky like Dad always does.

'In the clouds,' says Nanna suddenly, startling us. Her eyes stay closed.

The following day, Sunday, brings a soufflé of taunting cumulus but no rain. Dad paces and watches the wispy wheat and the sky. Galahs sleep all day in the old man mallee by the chook house. Mum sings in her garden. After tea, Dad lies on the couch, eyes shut. Nanna sits next to him with her hand on his forehead and rocks back and forth. She sings, *Rocking chairs and rocking horses, teddy bears and flying saucers…* But Dad's face is as closed as the clouds. Maybe he reckons the galahs have got the right idea, or maybe he's fed up with Nana Mouskouri.

Next day is the annual school cross country run. The route goes

across the oval, past the cemetery, and into the scrub along Lovers Lane
– a bush track snaking and switching with occasional tributaries into
secluded spots amongst mallee and broom bush. Then the lane stops
abruptly in the scrub. A thin foot track links it back to the school oval.

I can't win, so I don't think about that. There are too many athletes
in our school. The twins take winning in turns – it's Toni's this year.
But there's something about the race that thrills me. I think it's the
bush air and the sweat and the delicious aching in your legs when
you finish. Or that this is the one thing where I don't come last. Or
that Mum has driven into town with Nanna and they're waiting at the
finish line. My body is electric with strange tingles. I don't even feel
self-conscious with the spiky Beckham hairdo Nanna has given me.

We take off in a bumping panting bunch. By the time I get to
Lovers Lane, runners are stretched out like string and I am blessedly
alone. My body has settled into a warm electric rhythm, my brain on
time out. Trees hum above, a willy wagtail skips the air at my waist.
I run with my eyes half closed absorbing the humid twitching air. I
could run forever. *Rocking chairs and rocking horses…*

Later, I pass girls who stagger against trees, dripping and gasping.
Near the end of the lane, I come alongside the broad square shoulders
of Terri.

She gawks at me red-faced and sweating in glossy rivulets. 'Shit,'
she hisses as I pass her.

Ahead of her, the leading yellow T-shirted Toni looks back and sees
me coming, her long black hair waving down her back.

When I reach her, she looks down at me. 'Chicken Legs? What
happened to your hair? Hey, you look stuffed.'

The words shatter me. I don't belong here, my legs are too thin,
knobbly-kneed sticks with sudden pain locking them. I got them from
Nanna, along with the Beckham haircut. Toni is tall and cool, effortless
in her strong graceful frame, pretty face relaxed. Now I can feel the
rocks of my feet, the track slapping at them hard as brown concrete.
She flashes a smirk and glides ahead.

I keep on her tail but she is Toni and I'm a skinny bookworm, each breath screaming at me to stop and sit under a tree. There are times when I think I could pass her but she'll just laugh at me and speed up. We burst onto the oval and a gauntlet of kids cheer us over the line, me on Toni's heels. Nanna and Mum hug me and pour water on my head.

'Hey, I feel pretty good,' I blink out droplets.

'Good,' Nanna says.

'Did you see Toni?' Mum says, pointing.

Toni is flat on her back, groaning and being sprayed with water by her cooing mates. She coughs and orange vomit spills down her cheek. Teachers and a grey-haired St John's bloke hurry over. I stare. Could I have beaten her and she just made me think I couldn't? I'll never know.

That afternoon as I get off the bus, I'm still seething with unspoken anger at my lack of faith. Heavy clouds scud over head and I kick at the dust.

'Wish it would bloody rain!' My voice is an explosion.

'Don't swear,' says Mum, standing in the garden with Nanna.

'You'll win next year,' says Nanna, and Mum drops her trowel.

Nanna reaches out to me, grabs my hand. Then I notice they're both looking up at the house roof. Dad's braced with one leg on each side of the corrugated apex, shotgun tight in big hands, squinting up at the sky. A bandolier of red plastic shotgun shells hangs over one shoulder. The shottie has always been locked away, except when a fox comes after the chooks.

He's studying the goading clouds. This is it then; he's had enough of the drought, of watching the crop wither, the dam evaporate. He's gone mad. Stress. Drought syndrome. Nanna stares up at him, squashes my hand. Mum turns to us and I see one eye wink. Nanna's hand goes soft.

Dad points the gun at an especially bulbous bruise in the sky and the blast rocks our ears. He sways back in recoil, adjusts his feet. Galahs squeak awake, panic skyward and he waits for them to get out of the line of fire. Then he lets the clouds have it. BOOM BOOM. Hand pumping, barrel seeking the darkest patches. He stops to reload and I can hear him chuckling.

Nanna stretches my arm and hers up to the sky and she is laughing. Her silver hair, long and silk fine, washes against my face smelling of her favourite shampoo. A smell that always reminds me of the salon she used to have in town.

BOOM BOOM. Dad strafes the teasing mobs of locked-up water. Spent cartridges rattle onto the corrugations like rain and cascade into the gutters. He's seeding the clouds.

Then the ammo is gone and he climbs down the ladder. The muscles in his face twitch and glisten. He runs his palm over my spiky hair. 'Give us a hand getting those shells outta the gutters? It's gonna rain.'

'Gonna rain,' says Nanna.

Code

I'm really scared. I don' want to go to that stupid joint they call school but here's the big yeller bus parked at our stop and Mum kisses me and pushes me up the metal step. Dust follers me inside. The motor roars like it's inside the bus with us, makin' me jump. The bus shakes and takes off before I'm sat down and I get thrown into a seat. I look back and see Mum standin' on the side a the road gettin' covered in a cloud a white dust.

Then we're rattlin' long dirt roads. Bush an' paddicks goin' by through the bus winder. Look there's an emu an her chicks in the scrub. Look at the back of Gino's big head in the seat in fronta me. His black hair wet 'n' shiny. Afta ages, we hit the town bitchamin. The tyres hum. Brakes squeak. Door flumps open.

We clump down the steps. Look at the big yeller-painted buildings. People everywhere. I'm really really scared but I just follow Gino.

All the little farm kids have big worried eyes like they never seen this sort of thing before. Look at all the people, their big eyes say. Look at the yeller school! They must like that yeller colour. It's all over the place.

This place is just a big sea a cryin' and fuss. The biggest giant in the world's a blue lady yellin' her block off. Then she's parked over me. Her ankles are tree stumps and they have squiggly lines going all over them blue and red. These legs look like they growin' outa the ash felt. Up to a tree of wobblin' blue dress.

Me neck is frozen. Can't look up. Everythin' so big. I won' stay ere. I won'. Stupid shoes are tight. Never wear 'em at 'ome. Not stayin' 'ere in this yeller place. 'Maaaaaaaarrrrrrm!!!!'

I turn an' the sea a kids get out the road. Cripes, people start takin' notice when I start yellin'. 'Maaaarrrmmm, Maaaarrrrrm!' I run.

A coupla steps an there's a noise behind me an a claw crushes me arm. Jerks me flappin' inter the air.

I'm cryin'. I'm dyin'.

'That's enough of the water works!' The giant blue lady yells in me ear.

I'm flupped through the air an' plunked facin' the open yeller door. Me head is ringin'. Kids are shooed in roun' me. Don' they know I'm not stayin'? I don' belong here. I turn to run again. Blue lady knocks me in the head, spins me back inter the line. Where's Gino? I look long the line and see his shoulders and big head stickin' out 'bove all the kids.

Someone yells. Look. A little black girl. Red eyes. Bolts through a gap. Ha! She's made it.

Farm kids shuffle. Eyes blink with tears. Noses sniff for some free air, for their mums. Looks like me mum don't care. What's wrong with her? I think me arm is broken. I'll die here. Then she'll be sorry.

The blue lady's all around us, big arms wavin' 'n' flappin' like a windmill. She yells at mothers still hangin' round. Tells 'em they can go home.

Look at that tall bloke in a suit like a ploughed paddock, brown and wrinkled. 'N' how come he's got patches on his elbows? He must have a good mum who can fix up his old clothes. Look now. He's catched the little black girl with the red eyes. He's got her under his arm. She's hittin' at him but he's smilin' and talkin' to her soft like it don' matter. He comes an' helps whale lady herd us through the door. He's got a spongy voice and he don' yell. His hair is grey 'n' he looks just like that Harold Holt bloke that went swimmin' jus' before Christmas and never came back. It was on the wireless 'n' Mum showed me pitchas of him in the paper. Have to tell Mum later that maybe Harold Holt didn' drown after all.

Inter the room we go 'n' the whale lady is standin' at the front. She tells us her name is Mrs Joyce. 'Like James Joyce,' she goes.

Never 'eard of 'im. Can't be from round 'ere.

Lumpy letters go cross the top of a big blackboard. A pitcha of the Queen looks down at us from over the letters. She's a bit pale. After a while, we all go outside 'n' they shoo us inter lines like sheep. Harold Holt stands out the front on some sort of wooden platform and gets us all to sing for God to save the Queen. That's a good idea. I thought she looked a bit crook.

Mum 'n' Dad make me go to school the next day. An' the next day. They don' listen to me 'bout how stupid the joint is. Days 'n' days of it. So many they all go inter each other. But I learn some things.

I learn to do up me stupid shoelaces by meself. I learn you can get out inter the bright sunshine by sayin' you hafta go to the dunny. The dunnies are at the edge of the big ashfelt yard. Red brick an' grey sment. Only place in the school not painted yeller. Probly ran outa yeller paint. A shinin' smelly trough goes all long the wall. Sometimes if you're catched in there by a bad big kid, he'll walk past 'n' with a little push, send you inter the trough. Ony way to save yourself being to put out a hand on the sticky metal. So I try to go before recess or lunch. Get away from the yellin'. From the cryin' of the little black girl. Look out over the oval to the scrub an' paddicks. Wonder what's happenin' on the farm. I want to jus' start walkin' cross them paddicks 'n' go home forever. But Mum 'n' Dad'll make me come back. How can I get out of here? I dunno.

Above the dunny trough there's some square holes for windows. Too high for us little kids to see out.

One day, a big boy called Shrimp lobs a wee out of one. Then at lunchtime the contest is on. Boys line up, lean backwards. They stick their gobs over the sink taps and drink heapsa water. Practise. Up on toes. Leanin' back. Wee goes from their dicks in a big arc up and out through the windows. Splashes onter the ashfelt outside.

In the yeller room all day long, Mrs Joyce, her bum shakin', scratches at the blackboard with the chalk. The screechy noise makes horrible shivas down me back.

The black girl cries.

Mrs Joyce yells at her, 'No waterworks!'

One day, she hits the black girl on the hand with the ruler. The noise is like a gun goin' off. The girl stops cryin'. Look. She's cummin' out of her seat, eyes like cricket balls.

Mrs Joyce steps back. It's really weird but she looks frightened. 'No waterworks, I said!' Her voice is shaky.

A bit of yeller paint falls off the wall. The girl stands and stares at Mrs Joyce till Mrs Joyce turns and goes to the blackboard with her screechy chalk. She never cries again, that girl. And Mrs Joyce never hits her again.

For days on end, we all stare at the blackboard. Gino is the first to get it. Allovasudden, he starts readin'. His mum 'n' dad talk funny, but listen, Gino can read. He's goin' for it. I stare an' stare at the chalk letters, and Mrs Joyce yells at me.

Then…

It happens. Look. The scrawls on the blackboard formin' sumthin'. A small word comes from the board inter me head. Another. Another. A tiny sentence. I'm readin' an' I can't stop. I dunno how it works but it does, 'n' the more it does, the more it grows.

Days and weeks pass and whatever she screeches on the board I can work out. Mrs Joyce growin' smaller and my sentences bigger. I'm hungry for words round the room. The months at the top of the calendar. So many of them. Is a year in this place really that long? The metal plate stamped on the oil heater. Names on kids' pencil cases and bags. I can read. I can read.

Mrs Joyce gives Gino and me a shiny book about a coupla kids and a dog. Sends us out to the huge old tractor tyre under the big pepper tree.

A bit later, the black girl comes out with a book too. Smilin'. She waves her book at us like she won first prize at the town show. We make space on the tyre. Her name is Elizabeth. Like the Queen. We are three on a tyre swinging our legs and laughing at the kids and the dog in the book.

Harold Holt turns up in his brown patched jacket.

'What are you doing out here, children?' he says, sitting down on the old log in front of us. His mum has done a good job on his hair and it shines silver in the sun. He looks a bit worried.

'We're reading, sir,' says Gino.

'Yeah, we can all read now,' says Elizabeth.

A big grin splits his face. His teeth are white as the beach at Venus Bay. 'Really? That's a very big thing. A new world has just opened up for you, children. I'm very proud of you. Well,' he says standing up, 'keep it up.'

I run to the dusty bus every day. Some days, I see the emu family in the scrub through the bus window as we roar along the dirt roads. The chicks are growing. I want to read. I want to see Gino and Elizabeth and plan our adventures. They are full of stories. I can't get enough of stories. At home when I go to see Dad in the shed, he doesn't tell me any stories.

His favourite thing is to ask me, 'What do you want?' When I say 'Nothin',' he just holds out his closed fist opens it slowly and says, 'There you go: nothing.' Then he laughs like it's the funniest thing ever.

Gino's family is big. They have a big farm and big trucks that go to the cities all around Australia. Elizabeth doesn't know why they took her away from her family, though she says it's big too. I can't imagine being taken away from my family. Going home and not seeing Mum and Dad there. Going to the shed and hearing Dad's joke and then watching him fixing things. I think Elizabeth will read her way back to her family.

One day when we're reading outside on the tyre, Harold Holt comes and takes us to a room called a library. It's full of books and we can take them out. Take them home even. Can you believe it?

'You can choose,' Harold Holt says.

I'm collecting words that are my favourites. Library, holiday, reading. I borrow a big book. *Boys' Own Annual 1965.* On the front there's a picture of a bloke with long stringy black hair and a hat made of feathers. I slide my palm over his face.

Harold Holt says, 'That fellow's Geronimo. A very famous Apache. In America. You know, cowboys and Indians, the wild west and so on?'

'Apache…?'

That night, I read the book. It tells me those Apaches are wild savages. Hiding behind rocks, riding where they want to, ambushing cowboys. Outlaws, the book calls them. I decide I want to be an Apache when I grow up. Elizabeth, Gino and me will ride off on our spotted ponies, with our painted faces, barefoot and brave. All different colours. We'll go where we want. Just walking our ponies for the feel of the sun and the air. We'd ride out past the Gawler Ranges and who knows what we'll find. Might even find Elizabeth's family.

In another bit of the book there's a story about a code in the war. When the good side discovered the code, they found these boats that go underwater called submarines and the other side, the bad people, they couldn't figure out how the goodies knew.

I lie with Geronimo's stony old face looking out from under my elbow all night. I go to sleep in my home knowing I can be anywhere. My dreams are jumbled with everything that's old and new. Things I know and want to find out and a head full of stories. Adventures and people and history. Stories nearby and far away come and go in my dreaming head.

I dream I'm riding through the scrub on my painted pony but it's not any old scrub, it's Apache territory. The emu chicks have all grown up and I see them standing next to a funny-looking cactus with two arms. I dream Mrs James Joyce is walking on the asphalt past the boys' dunny windows at school. Somehow they've found more paint and painted the steel trough yellow to match the wee. I'm busting for a leak.

'How about some waterworks?' I say as I lean back and shoot my stream up and out of the dunny window.

Black Dogs Barking

It's dark and I'm busting. Yellow house light eddies from windows and over the back lawn like melted butter. Beyond the garden fence, in my head, I see the neatly trellised vines my grandfather planted, and try to think a way over the fence, along the edge of the vineyard, past the front of the house and the black dogs, to the stone toilet. The poo is pushing its way out and I squeeze it back in.

City kid in the country. Vines in the winter. Dressing the rolling hills in brown ripples. Blue sea on the horizon, burning scarlet in the sunset. The creek rushing and twisting through big gums. Kookaburras mocking like madmen. Dad on his pink and grey Massey Ferguson, back and forth all day amongst the rows with his bad temper. The little town with its stone buildings from the olden days, people I don't know who stop and say hello outside the shops in High Street.

And the black dogs. Nicky and King. Grandpa's dogs. They think they own the place, just waiting for him to come back. They guard the front gate at night, the path to the toilet, not knowing he will never come back. Best to have hope, I s'pose, to not know.

I want to cry. I wish we'd go back home to the big Unley house with its inside toilet, and no angry dogs. *Bonanza* on the telly. To my friend Trev across the street. Who will I sit next to in school here?

I sneak through the garden. A rose bush plucks at me, plants squelch and snails crunch beneath my bare feet. I climb over the fence, pushing down on the barbed wire, and into the clear lane at the edge of the vineyard. I think of Mum doing the washing up, ironing or something, listening to her Kamahl records. Dad in the shed belting at the plough with a hammer and his schoolteacher's hands, swearing

'It'll be all right once we get used to it,' he said when we came to live here a week ago. But only Mum, born here, is used to it. Not me, Dad or the black dogs. Everything is out of whack. I'm scared of school next week in the little old town of strangers who act as if they know me, and so scared I can't even go for a poo in the night. It used to be good to come here for holidays, before Grandpa died, before everything got stuffed up, before the black dogs smelt my fear.

So in the dark I begin my walk along the edge of the rows, touching the top of each fat end post for reassurance, like Grandpa used to do. 'Shiraz look good dis year, Grandpa, I tink,' I whisper to a post. The memory of him starts to cheer me up but I have to stay serious and quiet. Soon I will be parallel with the front gate, with the black dogs. I am a Comanche brave stalking a wagon train, so cleverly silent on my bare feet. Little Joe hunting down rustlers on the Ponderosa. Chips Rafferty watching over a mob of cattle. A bit more and I can turn left and out of the vineyard to the dunny. I can hear the crackle of the creek over the tops of the vines, the soft mumble of the ABC my Dad is listening to in the shed while he fights strange machinery.

Grandpa built the dunny when he was a young man starting up his block. Building and planting. When his toilet hole hit sheet rock beneath the rich soil of the valley, he chucked in gelignite, covered it with heavy rubbish that included an old broken bed complete with moulting mattress, and lit the fuse.

Mum was a small child then and still laughs when she tells the story about the bed shooting up, flat in the air, and hanging on the sky before crashing back to earth. 'Like you could sleep on it,' she said, 'floating on the clouds.'

'An air bed?' my dad added. Funny bloke, ha ha.

Anyway, the gelly blew a pretty deep hole. Grandpa made it into a long-drop dunny with a plank seat and squares of newspaper to wipe your bum. Now it's covered by a Twyfords flush toilet, and a roll of soft Kleenex toilet paper. Somehow I have to get to it and let this poo out. And soon.

Nicky and King, the black dogs, are pining for Grandpa but that's no reason to make my life miserable. I miss him too. In the holidays, he would sit me on his lap on the Fergie and let me steer. Prickles on his chin would tingle the back of my head, the smell of the soil and diesel in my face. The black dogs running behind, happily lolling pink tongues.

Grandpa wasn't tall and angular, like a movie star hero. John Wayne or Chips Rafferty. When I knew him, he was sort of small, knotted and strong like the vines, his bony legs digging into me on the tractor, his funny accent going in my ear.

'Shiraz she good dis year, Kit. Whatta you tink? Big wine. Eh?'

He would reach out a ropey arm and pretend to try and touch an end post as we went around to start another row. He wanted me to become his winemaker. And maybe one day I will, but first I'll put in an inside dunny.

Since we came here to live, I've tried going through the front gate to the toilet like Mum and Dad, very quietly, talking softly. But the dogs rise to their feet and begin their steady threatening growling. I try to go to the toilet only during the day, but every now and then I get caught out in darkness, like tonight.

The dogs don't bother anyone else at night. Mum and Dad walk boldly through, Mum gives them a pat, Dad swears at them. When Grandpa was alive and we came to stay for holidays, the dogs never minded anything. But they're messed up – scared and angry. They don't follow Dad and me on the Fergie. They mope along with Mum to collect the eggs, heads hung, eyes staring out. The rest of their days are at that front gate, like two barely sleeping killers, waiting waiting. They know I'm a scared skinny city kid. The more I know they know, the weaker and scareder I become. And the more they know it.

Brave Grandpa wouldn't put up with this. He jumped ship in Port Adelaide and swam to the shore in the night, just before his ship sailed. He worked for a builder in the city for a while, but he was a farmer at heart – he wanted land, that's what he had swum towards. Land. Always land. He wanted the feel of soil and the strong twist of growing vines in his days.

'Good country dis, our land,' he told me.

Our land. He was like a contented old king; his boundaries belonged to him, the fruit had his taste and wisdom. He had planted every post and every vine, tended each new bud, built the house and the dunny, helped by an Italian mate from Coober Pedy. Gelignite swapped for red wine – a good trade.

Grandpa died in the autumn, his last vintage safely beginning the journey to suppleness in its barrels. Old age, they told me. Well, I don't know about that. I think Grandpa just decided to go, like he always made his own decisions. I was with him in the cellar.

He sat in the old armchair sipping at a tasting glass of blood dark Shiraz, smudging his big grey moustache. 'You make wine dis gut one day, Kit. I tink so. Eh?'

I nodded from on top of an oak barrel where I lay spread out like a drying towel.

He swirled the glass, looked up at me and smiled. 'You good, Kit. Best ting ever grew here. You don' be scairt, eh?'

This was strange talk coming from Grandpa, I remember thinking. What's he on about? Then he emptied the glass, lay his head back and closed his eyes, a look of complete peace and contentment on his lined face. I didn't even know he'd stopped breathing, and I fell asleep on the barrel until Mum came and found us.

Soft breeze stirs the leaves of the creek gums. I shiver but I'm nearly there. My stomach is tight with the heady fear of my adventure. Bare foot falls on a stick. It snaps. A growl cuts the dark. Eerie and low. Questioning. Fear seeps from me like steam. More growls. My dark mind's eye sees Nicky and King getting to their feet. Snouts pointing. Unsheathing deadly daggers of teeth. I feel them padding towards me.

I turn and run. Barks like gunshots chase me through the chill air fast along the edge of the vines wind stinging my cheeks past the butter windows of the house to the low spot in the garden fence where I've bent the pipe crashing into the fence over into the tearing safety of rose bushes scrambling and dashing for the side of the house turning to see the flash of shining teeth at the fence angry barking fracturing the night.

'Shut up, you bloody mongrels,' Dad yells from the shed.

Thank God they won't come in the garden – they could easily leap the fence if they knew they were allowed to. I creep panting around to the back lawn, and the dogs stop barking, returning to duty at the front gate. It's only then that I feel the scratches all over me. Nothing digs and pulls like a rose bush. The need to poo comes back, more urgent. I want to cry. This is not fair. Not like on telly.

When all is silent, I head for the orange trees at the very back end of the garden, as far from the dogs as possible. In the leafy soil, I scrape a hole and find relief. I clean myself with handfuls of dried leaves. I am so miserable, so afraid. I think what Dad would say: 'You're shit-scared, mate!' or something like that. Funny bloke, ha ha. But he will never find out. Unless he goes for oranges and stands in the wrong spot.

That night in bed, I dream of fear, and a boy who looks like me. Standing on the deck of a ship, a frightened boy. Behind, rise its rust-smeared towers. In front, the lights of Port Adelaide blink at the rim of the continent. Though it's dark, memory pictures green meadows, seen over past days. Houses and wharves, an inlet. Hills rolling into purple heights. Strong joking men on the dock. Between fear and freedom, cold dark water. There is a rumble deep inside the ship. Soon the screws will engage and the journey back to Europe and its bickering kings will begin.

In a shirt pocket, wrapped in tar paper, is the square lump of a Bible. Say goodbye to the southern Appenines, brothers and sisters toiling all day in someone else's stony fields. The laughter and wine as they eat their midday meal amongst the vines. Ships in the Gulf of Salerno, filling a young head with visions of another world. The long walk to Napoli and a job on an ocean-going cargo ship. To Australia.

God give courage for this. Squeeze the Bible one more time, adjust the worn shoes hanging by laces around the neck. 'Don' be scairt,' a voice comes. Climb over the rail, and hang down, bare feet pointing to the water, the other hand on the shoes. Let go of the ship, and the fear, and slip into the waters of Port Adelaide.

The dream hangs in my memory vivid as sun over the valley.

A few days later, I'm caught again at night with the need to use the Twyfords and the soft paper. I stride to the front gate just as I have seen my mother and father do. In the light from the porch, the dogs rise, ready to kill. Nicky bares her teeth at me and King follows her lead. I smile at them, and swing open the gate.

'Hello, you black dogs,' I say, and they look up at me with grieving faces. 'Don' be scairt.' A firm pat, firm words, a friendly slobbering on my fingers and we're off up the path to the stone dunny built out of the earth by my grandfather's hands.

The Dog and the Fire

The superheated wind plucks at Rachel's grey hair. From a distant gully below the house, the smell of cindered pasture and vaporised eucalyptus oil swarms over the farm. She pats Jasper, her fingers touching the hard lump of scar between his ears. He licks her hand and whines deep in his chest. He knows she is afraid. He is her shadow always in all ways. A sheet of corrugated iron creaks and rattles from somewhere on the old implement shed, a hundred metres from the house. The power is off but she's connected the garden hose to the overhead tank that gravity feeds the house with rain water. The round sprinkler pulses a silver hoop of water where the lawn meets the thick shoulder-high diosmas that border the house.

'Come on, love,' she says to Jasper and they head down the stone path across the driveway to the shed and the fire pump next to the huge concrete rainwater tank.

The pump engine refuses to start. Rachel checks there is plenty of fuel. She can really feel the fire now. Smoke belches around the tank and over her. She pulls again and again at the starter rope. Nothing. The pump engine has been neglected. After her husband died, Rachel would start it once at the beginning of every summer to check everything was working, but for the last couple of years she's let it go. It was getting harder to stay on top of things.

'Start, you blessed thing!' She heaves again and again at the rope. Her right arm aches. Sweat slides off her forehead and drools across the lenses of her glasses, melts onto the plastic air cleaner cover of the engine. The crackling of igniting timber comes to her on the searing wind, the metallic cries of panicked galahs racing south cut the air.

She looks over the paddocks to the fire. She's shocked by how close it is now. Three kangaroos, one a joey, come leaping out of nowhere. They almost knock her over as they barrel past. A single bushy pine shrub that has somehow sprouted in the middle of the house paddock explodes before the flames reach it. She's been meaning to cut it down. If she'd asked Laura or her husband, they'd have come up from town and done it in a heartbeat. They're always offering to help. She resolves to take them up on it in future, be less independent. The main paddocks are leased out now, but the house, the sheds, the home paddock and her huge garden are getting tougher for her to look after on her own each year.

The pine disappears into smoke like a prop in a magic show.

She sweats over the pump engine for a dozen more fruitless pulls. 'Let's get inside.'

A fleck of something smouldering grey alights on her shoulder like a resting bird and she slaps it away. The path back to the house is paved with stone gathered from the paddocks a hundred years ago and the concrete holding it together is crumbling. Rachel and Jasper stumble up this path towards the shelter of the house. Her left boot catches a lip of stone and she goes down, feels the agonising snap of something in her left hip. When she tries to get up, the pain is beyond excruciating and she screams.

Jasper sniffs at her, electric with worry.

'I've had it, Jas. Can't get up. My hip. Get away love. Run. Go on.'

Rachel is eighty-eight, with the energy and vitality of someone half that. But not the body. No, she's got the worn-out hips; the mysterious bony aches that arrive without cause or reason. The creeping weight of time that she can no longer ignore.

Jasper examines her supine form, licks her face, figuring things out by taste and smell. In the smoke and boiling air, he takes the collar of her cotton work shirt in his teeth, makes sure he hasn't got any of her flesh and clamps down. He is not inured to the facts of his own frailty — that he is over a hundred in dog years, partly blind and deaf to all but shouts. But he ignores these truths and her protests, begins to drag her off of the path and onto the lawn. It's a real old-fashioned kikuyu lawn. Watered thick and green from the sweet bore. Not a timid scrap or, worse, one of those artificial plastic ones, but a dinkum lawn that says Welcome. Come in. Play here. And Jasper has played there for all but the first few weeks of his life.

Rachel found Jasper in the national park when she was on one of the bushwalks that she loves. It was winter. The mother dog and five puppies in a grim pile where they'd been tossed. They all seemed very dead till she saw the rise and fall of one puppy's chest in the tangled gore. The heartbeat of life beneath fur wet with the night's cold drizzle. She'd stuck him inside her coat, taken him home. He had a dented skull from the hammer blow that had been meant to kill him. She and Laura cleaned him up, dripped some calf formula into the little mouth and waited for him to die. He didn't. Now he's a big barrel dog of vague pedigree – kelpie intelligent, collie loyal, heeler tough – blue-grey with incongruous very white paint on his front paws.

He drags her across the lawn with her shattered hip through the burning sky towards the farmhouse door. His body trembles with the effort. Faintness envelopes him and he has to stop, concentrate on staying upright. After a moment, he continues. Another metre. His ancient lungs fighting for the oxygen in the smoke. Stops, rests, waits for the ricking in his arthritic legs to soften, wobbles on his shaking legs, goes again, dragging her bit by bit, closer to the solidity of the stone house and the little sprinkler circle.

Laura can see that the old house has somehow survived when she is still a kilometre away. Ashen dust smokes behind her car as she races along the dirt road. Firm corrugated roof and freestone walls emerge proud and whole amongst the black stalks and scorched earth of the farm where she grew up. It's an independent house, sturdy and belonging. She hits the brakes, begins to hope, her heart pounding, her nurse's fob watch bouncing against her chest as she leaps out of the car and runs. She is shocked by the devastated black earth, the ember redness of the sunset. Pallid ash mushrooms up from each footfall. But in front of her is a miracle. The old house is completely intact. The emerald lawn glistens coolly.

'Mum!' She runs along the crumbling stone path that winds across the haven of green. And then she sees the lump hidden behind the thick yellow diosma bushes by the front door. It's a body with Jasper spreadeagled on top of it. Still as stone. Next to them is a sprinkler. No water comes from it but the ground is damp.

'Jasper, oh God, Jasper.'

The big dog is on Rachel's chest, his dented head on her face. The puppy she helped nurse back to health so many years ago. Laura puts her hand on the dog's back and is struck by the rough singed feel of him, and by how cool his body is. Jasper is dead.

'Mum!' She pulls at Jasper. A voice roars in her head, leave him there, you don't want to see. But she goes on, lifts Jasper's body. All hair and bone. A life lived and given in faithful service.

The face revealed to her is pink. Laura is struck in that moment by how much her mother looks like her own new born granddaughter, despite the age difference. The beautiful unmistakable shape of the face. Behind the sweat-rimed glasses the big green eyes opening and looking at her.

Movement at the Station

In just his second year after graduation, Constable Lukas Ferdinand Schulz applied for a posting to a place so dangerous and hard to get to that he was the only applicant. Hence, they overlooked his youth and slight stature and gave him the job. They may have hesitated at his name but it was well before the war and industrious German settlers had pretty much kept the systematically planned but nonetheless faltering colony going in the early years.

Before he left Hahndorf, his parents commissioned a photographic portrait. In the South Australian Police Museum today, it portrays him as a stripling, but a very proud-looking one in a black uniform, the beginnings of a police-issue moustache on his baby face, the tip of his cavalry trooper sword well grounded.

With St Vincent's and Spencer's gulfs cleaving the interior and a dearth of roads, Lukas was conducted on the first part of his journey by sailing ship from Adelaide to Port Lincoln at the tip of Eyre's Peninsula (as it was titled in the possessive in those days – indicative of how European explorers and settlers saw this land). There he was issued with two police horses – a wiry impatient filly he named Flame because of a russet mane and tail, and a farting stocky piebald he called Gustav, after a similarly flatulent *Onkel*.

The sergeant in charge at Port Lincoln informed Schulz that the previous officer posted to Ellen had committed suicide with his revolver, a strictly forbidden use of a police firearm. The young constable was urged to note this regulation should he find himself in moments of lonely or alcoholic melancholy. The sergeant's tone suggested such a state of mind was not unlikely.

After dutifully imbibing unfamiliar rum with the local police, that night Lukas slept inadequately on a straw mattress that felt not so much straw as lumps of peninsula limestone. In the morning, he dressed carefully in his uniform, ensuring no wayward creases or bits of straw marred its magnificence. Later, he rode west away from the fine blue of Boston Harbour, glad to be alone with his sour head and his already beloved horses.

When he struck beach dunes some hours later, he angled north through intense squat scrub. He navigated by the sun and the coast, which varied from exquisite scimitar beaches to surf booming on blue-black rocks. On his landward side, unseen creatures shuddered and bounced through olive green. After midday, sap-stained sugar gums and stirrup high grass replaced the scratching scrub. When the horses inclined to dawdle, he stopped to let them graze and rest. He felt an urge to linger in this divine wild, his heart singing with both freedom and duty despite the headache of civilisation that also lingered.

There was no superior waiting at Ellen to log his time of arrival so he made a fire and apportioned himself considerable time over a cup of tea and a few slices of Hahndorf mettwurst.

In the late afternoon, the trio ambled through stony grey dirt mallee country, melaleucas and she-oaks of sandy coastal lowlands, salty malodorous swamps that thwocked at hooves, stands of twisted pale trees with bark like torn paper. Past Coffin Bay he rode into beautiful indents and out again to blinding beaches that pulled his soul into their mesmerising distance. Apart from two mad-looking fishers, he saw no humans, though he had a definite sense that people who knew this land were watching him. He would have been astounded to read the letters of the early planners who sight unseen had declared this country waste land.

On the inland side of a line of grassy dunes, he made camp and went to bed naked in his itchy grey police blanket, looking at blazing stars and listening to the hiss of the immense ocean. To the east, somewhere in the peninsula's heart, a dingo howled like a butcher's blade on steel. There were no replies. He thought of his mother and the other women under the same stars making the midnight walk through the eucalypt forests of the Mount Lofty Ranges, down from Hahndorf to Adelaide with their baskets of fresh vegetables, on the return journey up through the steep hills each basket carrying bricks for their new Lutheran church. That, he thought, would make a good sermon for stern Pastor Kloeden – along the lines of building something solidly good taking time and belief and a lot of dogged mountain climbing.

The following day he was dawn ready, his head blessedly clear of police rum. In the optimistic morning light, he rode along cliff tops, straight-backed as if on parade. Though he practised a Pastor Kloeden like expression, his heart was smiling and the smooth planes of his right face were lit in sunrise gold.

On his left, so breathtaking were the gnawed cliffs that he shivered at their magnetic pull, imagining himself plummeting through mist to the shattering surf below. As he rode, he studied a white blur on the sea horizon but could not discern if it was a sailing ship or a cloud

The next sapphire afternoon, his reverent journey was shattered when he smelt woodsmoke and saw unnatural shapes on a ridge far ahead. The tiny settlement's presence was announced by the word 'Ellen' in white stones on the ground. Low buildings were slung haphazardly above an elongated bay. The entire place was incongruously ugly – a contradiction to his recent immersion in beauty. At the sea mouth of the bay, he noted the dark line of a submerged rock bar and a regular swell foaming over it.

The two-roomed wattle and daub police hut with its pounded dirt floor and musty odours dented his pride in his new posting only momentarily. Behind this building was a tiny stone structure with a low door of iron bars, and iron rings and chains mortared into the walls. It smelt eye-wateringly of piss and shit. The jail cell. The other main building in the settlement was a short way along the ridge, its title proclaimed in a wooden sign lettered with white paint as if by a child – the Sportsman's Arms. Lukas had not seen what he would call a sportsman since he left Adelaide, and the big fellow who waved at him from the pub door didn't appear to fit the bill.

As he was unloading the horses, the publican wandered up. 'G'day, mate,' the man said, adjusting his trousers around his fat waist as if surprised at the tightness of their fit and touching his forehead. Receiving no return salute, he shoved out a hand and Lukas shook it.

'Good day, sir. Constable Lukas Schulz.'

'Bryson Tennant, publican. Schulz? German that is, isn't it?' He sucked through a gap in his brown teeth. 'Any rate, welcome. Anythink you need, I might be able to help. Come over for a drink, won't you?'

Gustav shook his head and farted wetly. Flame snorted and ambled away. 'Not just now, thank you. I'd like to get my gear inside and settled in.'

'All right. Well, maybe tomorrow evening? Prob'ly even be a boat in. A bit of company.'

'Thank you.'

'Hope you have more backbone than the poor bugger you're replacing. The blacks around here need a firm hand. This country will prosper once we make it safe by showing the bastards who owns the land.'

'I will uphold the law, if that's what you mean.'

'Of course, lad. That's what I meant.'

Lukas carried water from the communal well, washed carefully and dressed in his one set of civilian clothes. He brushed and cleaned his uniform meticulously and hung it in the flimsy wardrobe. He was keen for the dawn so he could put it on again and continue the dour sense of work and duty imbued in him by Silesian peasant parents and the free colony that had welcomed them.

In the morning, he was eating breakfast inside when his door was emphatically pounded on by a shock-faced white-haired sheep farmer. The man explained that something had happened to one of his shepherds. He directed the constable to a well-worn horse trail heading inland. Lukas gleaned the details, threw a saddle on Flame, and trotted her into the scrub. Bryson Tennant and the sheep man followed.

Lukas came upon the shepherd's hut backed into an elbow of a little creek. It was a hovel of roughly cut native pine logs, the gaps between plugged with flaking mud that still bore the builder's finger dents, its roof a puzzle of tree bark. The miserable room contained a small wooden table, a single knocked-over chair, and an iron cooking stove. There was a shelf along one wall holding nothing but dust. No food, no cooking implements or homely accoutrements. The place looked fairly well cleaned out. Frayed jute rope knotted and tangled around a knobby wall post reminded Lukas of the iron chains in the police cell.

The headless shepherd was lying on his belly next to the stove, arms underneath as if keeping them warm. The man had very short legs so that without his head he was almost as wide as long. Lukas lifted his hat and wiped sweat from where its rim had dented his forehead. Mumbled grunts and hissed threats of murder and being murdered reached him and he turned to see Tennant glowering. The sheep man had retreated outside. Something, police instinct probably, drew Lukas to the iron stove.

The human head inside so stunned him that he slammed the oven door shut and stepped back, stumbling as a boot heel caught an imperfection in the dirt floor. He swallowed and closed his eyes, reminded himself of his sworn duty.

When he opened his eyes, the stove grinned at him as if enquiring whether he had the balls to open the oven door again. He leaned forward, arching his body like he wanted to stay as far from what was inside as possible. The steel handle turned and screeched and he stepped back, letting the heavy door fall open and clang off its hinges.

The head looked out at him, open-eyed, brown-bearded, startled.

'God save us all,' said Tennant.

'You may go back now, sir. I'll oblige you to keep this to yourself until I respectfully deal with the body and I've informed Adelaide.'

'What about the fecking savages? Just because he…'

'He what, Mr Tennant?'

The sheep man stood at the door wringing his hat in big hands. 'He stole one of the native girls. Had her tied up here. I heard about it and came out to give him the boot and take her back to her people. I know them, speak some of their language. The Naou. But I was too late…'

Tennant put his hands on his hips. 'I'll get some blokes and horses together and we'll teach those bastards.'

'You will do no such thing, Mr Tennant. I'll put in a report, the police will investigate and send a patrol to catch the perpetrators. Then they'll get a fair trial.'

The sheep man shook his head again. 'I told him not to interfere, to respect them…bloody idiot.'

Tennant was red in the face. 'A fair trial? This isn't Adelaide or feckin' Berlin, mate. We won't get new settlers here if they get away with this.'

Lukas thought he might point out the South Australian Letters Patent Act guaranteeing the rights of native peoples to lands now actually occupied or enjoyed but correctly deduced he would be wasting good breath. 'Please depart, Mr Tennant, or help me carry the body back to Ellen. Which do you prefer, sir?'

'All right, constable, I'll go. But we've a right to protect our lives and property from murdering heathens.'

'I'm sorry, lad,' said the sheep man, worrying his hat back on his woolly head. 'I have to get back to my family.'

It was a long way to carry the corpse to Ellen on the back of Flame, and the constable wondered how you manage a body and a detached head on a flighty horse anyway. He found a small grassy meadow in a paperbark copse nearby. He undressed to underwear and boots and hung his uniform neatly among tree branches. The soil was sandy and using a tough slab of bark from the hovel's roof he eventually scraped a trench mid-thigh deep. He struck sheet limestone and could go no further, not without explosives. It was getting late and he did not want to be within cooee of this place at night.

The head unstuck reluctantly when he reached into the oven. He held it out in front of him thinking of drips on his boots and walked quickly back to the grave, placing it at one end of his trench.

He dragged the body out and flopped it in. A little gut-churning rearranging and in the failing light the body looked acceptably whole. When done, he washed his hands in the creek, cleaned himself up with a meticulousness his mother would commend and put on his uniform.

Back at the grave, he held his hat to his chest, bowed his head and said the Lord's Prayer aloud, hoping God would forgive him for hurrying the trespass and trespassing bit, feeling all the time that he was indeed doing just that.

Flame was as keen to get out of there as he and commenced a furious gallop the moment his backside hit the saddle.

The following morning gloomed under a sky at the edge of weeping. A whaler sat at anchor inside the bar as if welded onto a rigid sheet of blue metal. Along the coast to the north, a cloud rope of smoke connected earth to sky.

Men clumped up the coastal path to the pub, grunted and cursed through plans of retributive adventure, while eyes cast wary glances towards the police station and the northern smoke. The flame-maned chestnut and the piebald snoozed standing up in the horse paddock. The feeble buildings of the station and its boyish strutting constable were laughable to these men of axes and blade ploughs, rolling decks and whales the size of a ship that take a long time to die.

It wouldn't be long and the young bloke would have to ride the news to Port Lincoln; no one else would do it. All could now claim a need to protect their family and property.

Lukas spent the day writing a very neat and detailed report and afterwards going about and entreating the near homesteads and the whalers hanging around the pub but none would be his messenger of police.

That night, the watchers saw no movement at the station, but there was plenty going on inside the constable's young head. A head short on experience but long on belief in duty and laws both written and heartfelt.

Just before dawn, he saddled Flame and headed south towards Port

Lincoln. The lookout noted that he was travelling light and fast on that undersized racehorse. The beat of hooves on the rough and broken ground had not long faded when a caustic organism quilled with gun barrels began to form outside the Sportsman's Arms.

The district was sparsely populated, even if they counted the Naou, which they most certainly did not. That perfectly adapted sovereign first nation and its many millennia of history were no match for papers of ownership.

With locals and whalers, the Sportsman's gang grew to eight men, a veritable horde in these parts. Nearly all the cracks had gathered to the fray. There was Tennant of course. Clayton from Mount Wedge came down to lend a hand, bringing his most ruthless shepherd with him. Neither was averse to using whip and rifle, or handouts of strychnine-laced flour. In fact, they were proud of it. Much better than wasting good land on them like the colonial government did over at Poonindie on the peninsula's east coast.

They made plans, washing down the details with ample rum. The Naou smoke they could see was coming from a patch of scrub at the edge of the beetling cliffs to the north. That was handy. The cliffs and the pounding sea would clean up the job nicely. No bodies would ever tell the story of their ride.

The riders neared the Naou camp around midday. They were electrified by adrenalin, alcohol, the self-righteousness of conquest, and sure triumph. The Naou at that time were depleted by poison and European diseases, murder and dispossession. The numbskull primitives didn't have guns so all you had to do was stay out of spear range, laughed Clayton, the expert in this kind of venture. Ride and whoop and shoot a few bucks and the rest will start running – then you must wheel them, wheel them for the cliffs, boys.

The bush fairly rang as Clayton led their brave gallop into the clearing. But there they all took a pull, hooves sending the lime stones flying.

In the middle of the spear grass meadow was a mounded fire, thick smoke generated by deliberate green branches ravelling upward in the fat still air. The Naou were not visible but they were watching in the ringing scrub, hardwood spears honed and fire tempered to rib piercing keenness.

Next to the fire stood the snow-haired sheep man trying to aim a repeating rifle. Its barrel mouth pointed alternately at the horses' hooves and the clouds. A few feet from him on a flame-maned horse a straight-backed crisply uniformed stripling glared along the sights of his police issue Martini Henry carbine, his aim steadfast on Clayton's chest.

Fault

Neil looked out over the service station forecourt and its dusty bowsers standing to attention in the fluorescent lights. He liked the early morning shift. From his console, he felt in control again, like a pilot in a cockpit surrounded by important switches, gauges and flashing LEDs. For the first time in years, he was able to forget his shame for a few hours. It was therapeutic to look out through the big windows and watch the sprawling town come awake, to see hope-filled light creeping into the world. He loved seeing the country sunrise washing the wide streets in orange light, the new day burning the past further away. In an hour or so, the highway traffic would build. Mine vehicles were becoming common these days. As well there were the usual farmers, grey nomads and truckers, and later people off to do the shopping or whatever, all with a purpose, money in their pockets. And out here none of these people knew what he'd done.

A motorbike pulled up silently outside the front windows by the gas bottles. He peered at the grainy grey image on the CCTV monitor, his heart leaping as he recognised the bike. It seemed to be an original Honda CB750 just like the one he'd lost all those years ago. Those beautiful bikes were now collectors' items. The rider had already dismounted and was walking slowly towards the doors of the servo. They shucked open and the man hesitated as if unfamiliar with automatic doors, before entering with his boots shuffling on the lino floor.

Neil smiled across the counter at the old full-face helmet and scuffed leather jacket. 'G'day mate. Um, might get you to take that helmet off if you don't mind. Sorry, company policy, you know…'

A gloved hand thumbed up the helmet's tinted visor. Aviator sunglasses looked out. How the heck could this bloke actually see anything at this time of the day? Neil thought. Some people…

Then the other glove shakily unfolded a note on the counter and a leather finger jabbed at the words printed in bold on it: I'VE GOT A GUN GIVE ME ALL TEH MONEY

Neil gasped and looked up. He didn't think it was a good time to point out the typo on the note. 'Cripes! You serious?'

A pistol appeared and pointed at Neil's nose.

The helmet cleared its throat and said, 'Um, sorry, please hurry.' It was an old voice, perhaps around Neil's own era, gritty, gloomy, trembling.

Neil hit the till with his fist. The draw shucked open. They'd never had a hold-up and didn't expect one. Security consisted of the ring of keys Neil had been given to open up at five a.m. and the pathetic CCTV monitor.

He didn't want to be shot in the face by a nervous old biker who might not even be able to see him clearly. He'd have to appease him with the float in the till. It wasn't much, with most customers these days paying by card. Neil slid out the few notes and coins and pushed them onto the counter. Gloved fingers flicked clumsily through them, and they disappeared into a pocket of the leather jacket. The pistol wobbled at Neil's chin.

The gloomy voice trembled again. 'Um, the safe? Could you open it please?'

Neil shrugged and tried to look apologetic. 'Can't, mate. I don't know the combination. The owner will be in soon.'

Neither of those things were true but maybe it would make the bloke clear out.

'Oh,' the helmet twisted around anxiously, scanning the deserted forecourt and the servo doors, the pistol waving at the ceiling, the drinks fridge, the pie warmer, the racks of almost out-of-date chips. Neil saw that the chamber of the pistol above the trigger was missing and pocks of corrosion dented the remaining metal. The sunglasses were looking at him again, the pistol hovering around his neck region.

'Well, I, I expected a bit more. It's not enough to pay our...'

There was resignation in the voice, defeat, feelings Neil was very familiar with.

'Look, maybe take a few chockies or something?' Neil offered.

The helmet looked along the row of confectionery, the pistol barrel sagging downwards. If the thing could actually fire, it would blow a hole in the counter and probably Neil's balls. A Cherry Ripe was selected and brought up to the sunglasses with a shaking hand.

'I love these things but, er, nearly a thousand kilojoules. What's that in calories? I've gotta be careful with my diet, Anne says.' He put the Cherry Ripe back and picked up a Crunchie, again peering at the back of the wrapper, before putting it quickly back as if he'd read cyanide in the list of ingredients. 'No, thanks.'

'Well, what about a chocolate frog? They're only sixty calories and if you buy four you'll get two cents a litre off your fuel, if you wanna fill up. Er, not that you'd be paying…'

The hand holding the gun was now resting on the counter, as if the weapon had become too heavy. It was aimed at a bowl of overpriced fruit.

'Could I have one of these bananas here? They're healthy.'

'Help yourself.'

'Thanks.' The voice seemed to brighten a little at this small win. 'I need to get my money's worth, so to speak. It's been so hard since, well…'

'Since?'

'Look, mate, I'm not a bad person. I got sucked in by a bunch of pricks called Paramount Investments. You may have heard of them? The returns were so good in the early years I talked Anne into borrowing against our house and investing more, to set us up for a good retirement, and something to leave our grandchildren. Well, when the GFC hit, they went bust and it all vanished. The bank took our house, everything. Can hardly keep up the rent on our little unit now with this so-called mining boom taking over the district and driving prices through the roof.'

'I lost…' It was Neil's turn to have the shaky voice. He was in shock. 'Well, er, I…I fell on hard times too.'

'At least you've got a job to go to.'

'I was lucky, I'm related to the owner of this joint,' said Neil. 'After two years of trying, I couldn't get a job anywhere except out here. My cousin owns this service station.'

Neil's former boss, the CEO of Paramount Investments, had only recently gotten out of jail, a fate Neil narrowly avoided by not actually having broken any laws that they could find, though he had been banned from the finance industry for life.

'It's hard to get a job at our, er, my age. People think we're past it, when we've actually got years of life experience and wisdom to offer.'

The helmet nodded. 'It's age discrimination, for sure. Our state manager always said I was one of her best people, but a few months after I was made redundant, they laid her off too. An American hedge fund or something bought the firm, management moved to Sydney and they employed young people on new contracts.'

'Our experience, our work ethic, all means nothing,' said Neil. 'And we're not that old.'

'Not old, just mature. And everything's so expensive now. It's a two-speed economy all right, but some of us are stuck in blimmin' neutral. They're threatening to shut off our electricity if I don't pay something off the bill by tomorrow, and I've got rent due and Anne's cancer has come back. I know it's from stress, and it's all my fault. I got greedy. She was against us going into Paramount's scheme but I wouldn't blimmin' listen.'

Neil knew about greed, and about fault. He didn't remember this bloke, understandably with the sunglasses and helmet hiding the face, but he'd talked people just like him into mortgaging their house to invest in Paramount's high-risk high-return schemes. In his defence, he'd genuinely believed everything his boss, the Paramount CEO, had told him. Or to be truthful, he'd turned a blind eye because he wanted to believe that the good times would go on forever. He even invested his own entire healthy savings and indeed the returns were outstanding for a couple of years – then it all disappeared.

'Look, I hope this won't get you into any trouble,' said the helmet.

'I'll be all right. You've got a gun. What could I do?'

'Oh, this old thing?' He lifted the pistol off of the counter and turned it to show Neil. 'It's not loaded. And it's got no firing pin. It was my grandfather's. He was an officer in World War 1. Killed by an artillery shell on the western front. His best mate somehow smuggled it back, gave it to the family. Anyhow, I better get going. I'm sorry about all this, mate.' He put the banana back in the bowl.

Neil nodded towards the Honda gleaming on the forecourt. 'Nice bike you've got there. Used to have one just like it myself. Candy red.'

The bloke stopped in his tracks. 'Yeah? The candy red, eh? She woulda been beautiful.'

Neil noticed the tremble in the voice had been replaced by a spark. The shoulders were suddenly set more square in the leather jacket, the back straighter.

'Yeah. Bought it new,' Neil explained. 'Had it until 1983 when it got burnt to a melted skeleton in the Ash Wednesday fires.'

'Cripes! Destroyed totally?'

'Yeah. We were renting an old farmhouse in the Adelaide Hills. I'd just been moved to head office at the bank and my wife was home with our two-year-old son and the bike was in the shed. I'd taken the train into the city. Lost everything.'

'Everything? What do you mean? Your family, they got out okay?'

'No. When I say everything, I mean everything but the clothes on my back and a few photos I kept at work. When they let me back onto the property, all that was left was twisted iron, and the carcass of the bike sitting like a white ghost in the ashes. But I was beyond caring about the bike by then.'

'Blimmin' hell, I'm so sorry, mate.… I don't know what to…' The helmet bowed towards the ancient pistol. It turned guiltily in the gloved hand, as if he wanted it to disappear.

'Don't worry about it. It was a long time ago. I've had a few bikes since then, and a few girlfriends too, but there's nothing like that first love.' Neil realised he was talking about his wife, not so much the candy red Honda. Back then, he'd had everything a man could want, including his integrity. It had been the best time of his life. And now he also realised that they'd been relatively poor in financial terms, just like he was now.

The bloke went silent, the sunglasses staring at Neil. Then he jerked a gloved thumb back towards the forecourt. 'Er, would you like to have a look at her?'

'I'd bloody well love to,' said Neil.

'What about your boss?'

'The boss? Oh, he doesn't come in till after lunch.'

Under the glaring white fluoros of the servo forecourt, they marvelled in silence at the gleaming machine. A candy gold CB750. Neil was reminded of the day he'd walked into the showroom and laid eyes on his own candy red. It was his eighteenth birthday and he'd just been made permanent as a teller at the local bank branch. He'd been in a mood to celebrate and immediately fell in love with the distinctive louvred side covers and hump in the seat, the lustrous powerful-looking engine, the way the thing started almost before the salesman hit the button. Then the perfectly balanced hum of those four cylinders singing of the open road, calling him to twist the throttle. He'd paid a deposit on the spot, knowing he was eligible for a cheap staff loan through the bank.

His reverie was interrupted by the owner of the candy gold.

'Bought her brand-new in Sydney in 1969, before Anne and I got married. Knew I had to get her then or I never would. Hung onto her through all those temptations and pressures to sell. Mortgages, kids, you know…er, sorry.' The bloke's voice throttled down to a murmur, and he changed gear quickly. 'Have to sell her now, though, got no choice. Went into the library and put her on the internet a coupla weeks ago. Had a few calls but no one's been prepared to do the drive out here. I'm kinda relieved every time that happens, as if the distance is protecting me, giving me an out from selling, even though we're desperate. When she's gone, well, it'll break my heart, but we're on the bones of our arse at the moment, as you can tell. Can't even afford to put petrol in her these days. This is the first time she's been out of the shed in a year.'

'Well, the bike's an absolute credit to you. Isn't there any way you can keep it?'

'I've tried everything, mate, believe me. But I can't seem to get a job at my age, and my wife's, well…'

Neil suddenly remembered something. 'Hang on, my cousin mentioned he's thinking about extending our opening times. With the mining boom around here, there's vehicles coming and going at all hours. As soon as he can find good staff, he said. And that's not as easy as you'd think. There'll probably be a part-time job opening, if you don't mind working a few hours at night. He's a good boss and he pays above award for good people. I could have a word with him.'

'Really? That's…well, I, cripes, after me sticking a gun in your face you'd do that for me?'

'Some things are not our fault. Drop off your details later and I'll put in a good word. The owner likes us mature types, reckons we know how to work, that they don't make 'em like they used to.'

Neil and the bloke looked at each other and the Honda, and they both understood.

'I don't know how to thank you. A few hours work at nights would be perfect. It'll keep our heads above water and the bike with me where she belongs. Here, take this money back.' He scrabbled in his jacket pocket and guiltily put the crumpled notes in Neil's hand. 'Er, I suppose the job will be safe? Don't servos sometimes get held up at night?'

'Out here? Nah. We've never had a hold-up, ever.'

Little Islands

'Gettin' any bites?' John said, asking the obvious.

'Nah. You?'

'Not yet.'

The sun had drifted behind a patch of fat clouds hovering over Cape Bauer. But it was still hot out in the bay.

'Maybe we should try somewhere else?'

'Right. There's whiting about, all we gotta do is find 'em.'

Good, I thought. We were finally going to fish somewhere other than Little Islands. The tyre reef would make a nice change. John always took me fishing here at Little Islands. We rarely caught a lot but it never bothered him. He was an optimist.

'Maybe on the other side of the islands,' he said after a few moments of thought.

I rolled my eyes but didn't argue. We started the outboard and chugged to the other side of the furthest of the guano-streaked rocks called Little Islands, found a patch of clear bottom, dropped the anchor, baited up and cast out.

Twenty minutes later, we hadn't had a bite. A south-westerly breeze sprang up. Small waves slapped against the jagged shores of the islands and drummed at the aluminium sides of the tinny.

'That breeze is coming up, John. Do you think we oughta head on home soon?' I said.

'No worries, mate. We'll go when we've caught a few. It's gonna happen. I can feel it.'

'Righto.'

But the fish didn't bite. We drank the last beers and tried several other likely looking spots around Little Islands. The wind was making the tinny pull and sway on the end of the anchor rope like a newly caught brumby. I kept looking hopefully at John but he was intent on his line, reeling it in and studying the bottom before throwing it out, over and over again.

Finally he sensed my nervousness about the breeze and the chop that was slopping into the boat hard enough to lift spray. 'Righto, mate, one more cast, then we'll get outta here… Cripes!'

Something big latched onto John's line, so hard and sudden it banged his hand into the aluminium gunwale. Simultaneously I felt a massive tug on my line. In moments, we were each reeling in a sleek whiting. We cast out again and I felt that firm hungry fish tug on the line immediately. We pulled in fish after fish. The esky was soon the way it should be at the end of a fishing trip – empty of beer and full of fat King George whiting. Then, as if a switch was turned off, the bites stopped. We both sat there, tweaking our lines, pulling them in and recasting, but the whiting had gone.

John was exultant. 'Cripes, that was great. I told you – Little Islands is the spot.'

'Sure was, but look at the bay!'

The sea was flecked with white caps. The shore far to the south, where the town and boat ramp are, was lost in a mist of sea spray coming off the rocky edges of the islands and the tops of wind slashed waves.

'Cripes,' he said. 'But listen, I have to take a leak before we get going.'

'Me too.'

We leaned, wobbling and hanging on, with our dicks over opposite sides of the tinny. I heard him start but the rocking movement of the boat more than cancelled out the pressure in my bladder. I concentrated on relaxing and not thinking about drowning but it was impossible, so I gave up.

The outboard refused to start. We took turns pulling at the starter rope but the motor made only discouraging fluffing sounds. Waves started to come over the bow. I wondered how long it would take for someone to come and rescue us from a perch on the nearest island. The white and grey streaked serrated shores did not look comfortable.

'Let's get this cover off and see what's upsetting this baby,' said John, patting the engine. 'I reckon there're some tools in a plastic bag up the front there, under the life jackets.'

I found the tools quickly – a couple of rusty screwdrivers, a spark plug spanner and a small ancient shifter wrapped up in an old bit of yellow plastic.

We finally got the spark plug out. It was very oily-looking and John cleaned it on a dry bit of his T-shirt. With it back in, the motor fired immediately and after a few introductory smoky rattles, settled into a healthy-sounding burble. Up with the anchor and we were off.

As we came around the island to head for Streaky Bay town, we were hit head on by the powerful southerly and a vicious chop that hurled water into the boat. I looked over at the eastern shore and began to calculate distance and probable swimming time. We were going down, definitely. I grabbed a life jacket and threw one back to John.

But John, his hand wrapped around the twist throttle of the outboard, grinned at me through the spray as if he was a kid at Sea World. To reassure me, he put one arm through the life jacket. The motor screamed over the sound of the waves hammering into the metal hull. I looked towards the shadowy grey bumps of the town in the distance. A shape appeared from the west and sped out into the bay. It was a windsurfer, the brightly coloured triangular sail dipping and flashing over the top of the water at an incredible speed. Far above and to the south, the stark white trail of a jet appeared briefly in a blue gap between the clouds. Those things of normality and John's grin made me decide that we were going to make it, that there was nothing to worry about.

Then the shrill of the motor suddenly disappeared and the tinny stopped as if shot. A big wave smacked into us, almost throwing me over the bow. I turned and John was gone. The back of the tinny was empty. I scrabbled for the anchor and threw it over.

Then I saw John's dark head bobbing amongst the wind torn waves. Clutched in one hand was the life jacket. He waved it at me and grinned.

I pulled and pulled at the starter rope, without effect. Spray came over the bow like driven rain, soaking me and the engine as I pulled the lid off. Skinning my knuckles, I removed the hot spark plug. It was black with oily gunk.

'You've got the mixture too rich!' I yelled, but no one answered.

John was gone.

I cleaned the plug as best I could and quickly screwed it back in. I found the fuel mixture screw and turned it a little, hoping I'd gone the right way. The motor started immediately, and I upped anchor and spun the boat back towards the islands.

I found him a few moments before he was about to be pummelled into fang-like rocks at the shore of one island. Slewing alongside, I grabbed his arm and with a lot of grunting on both our parts, slid him up over the gunwale and into the boat.

'The water's nice once you get used to it,' he coughed.

I spun the bow around, gunned the motor and headed for the nearest beach.

'Hey, mate, where are you going?' he called. 'Town's thataway.'

'Blow that, mate. We'll never get there in this sea.'

'Come on. This is nothing. Gis the rudder. No point walking home when we can drive.'

At that moment, a windsurfer raced across our bow, skipping from wave to wave like a bolting kangaroo.

'We're filling up with water.'

'We'll be right. We want to get these fish home and in the pan.'

We smashed our way back through the middle of the bay, dodging several windsurfers who stitched their way back and forth across our path.

After a hammering and lurching journey and carrying a significant portion of the ocean in the bottom of the tinny, we pulled into the deserted boat ramp. I leapt off and ran behind a bush for a leak.

Later as we winched the tinny onto the trailer John said, 'That was bloody good fun. And we caught fish.'

'All's well that ends well, I suppose,' I said.

'Little Islands,' he said. 'Told you it was a great fishing spot. We should go out there again next weekend. What do you reckon?'

'Righto.'

How To Grow Tall In One Season

We have try-outs for team selection three nights in a row, down at the netball courts by the footy oval. Just like last year. At the first try-out, I drop easy passes. The club president is watching. A stare like a slips catcher, Dad reckons. Makes me shiver with fear every time the ball comes. My hands know it and keep fumbling. I try to make up for it by running around a lot.

The next day, Dad goes into hospital. Again. I can't concentrate at school. Keep thinking about everything he's been through. Hospitals and operations. Surgeon making a mistake with the nerves so he can't move his fingers. Another surgeon trying to fix it. Dad not being able to do his plumbing business, his van getting dusty in the shed. Then Mum's cancer. That trumped everything. Forget the shoulder. Forget everything else.

I run all the way from school to get to the second try-out because the teacher keeps the class in. I'm worn-out and late. The president looks at me like she's stepped in dog poo.

The only good thing is Dad being home when I get there after. He's slumped on the lounge, sling armed, hand a fat fist of bandages. There's some kind of plastic thing along his forearm. It's till the nerves wake up. If they ever do, he explains. His voice is old and tired. That scares me. Dad never gives up.

At the last try-out, my passes go great. But the president isn't even looking. Standing next to her is our coach from last season, Lizzy. They look like they're arguing about something.

We go to the clubrooms afterwards to hear about the teams. Our age group sits together on the beer smelling carpet. Just like last year. The president is going on and on. The club is growing, she reckons.

Lots of new houses in town. A huge farm swallowing up littler ones in the valley. Lettuces for fast food. McDonald's Farm, Dad calls it. I look at a long speckled cigarette burn like a grub in the carpet. I think about Dad sitting at home on his own, not being able to work.

I look at my friends. At least I've got them.

First they put the A grade names on the big screen.

The president is captain again. 'My tenth year in a row,' she goes.

As if we didn't know.

It takes ages for them to get down to the juniors. My mouth goes gluey. The president says there will now be two divisions in juniors. They tell us the coach for division 1. It isn't Lizzy. Maybe because she's doing year 12 this year she isn't going to coach again.

Then they put the Juniors div 1 names up. All my friends. But not me. I can't believe it. An ache pumps up in the back of my head and pushes against my eyes.

They put div 2 up. There are kids I know and some strange names. And me. At the bottom. Rachel the short arse. And Lizzy as the coach.

The cigarette burn in the carpet is rough and hollow. I sausage my little finger into it.

The president is talking again. Just like last year she goes, 'Who wants finals or fair?' She shoves her fist in the air and yells, 'Finals!'

The air fills with raised fists. 'Finals!' They sound like blowflies stuck at a window.

But this year I don't join in. I see Lizzy doesn't either. When the president says 'fair' she puts the palm of a hand over one ear and shakes her head. Everyone plays her game and stays quiet, just like last year. I want to put my fist up and yell what about unfair? But I'd never be brave to do anything like that. Not with that lump at the back of my eyes.

I can't look at anyone. I stare at the photos along the red-brick wall of the clubrooms. There's Dad's footy team from last year just after they won the grand final. Everyone has their arms folded except him. He couldn't. That final, the last game he ever played, was the one his shoulder got smashed. We all thought that was a disaster, but it was nothing compared to what happened to Mum, to us.

After the meeting, walking up the hill to town, I start crying. I feel sick. And then ashamed for being such a cry baby. I want Mum so bad. My heart can't let go. I'll never let go of her.

How can the world be so unfair? And now I'm dropped. You're just not good enough, that's what they're saying. I know it's because of my stupid height.

When I get to the top of the grassy hill, the street lights are flickering on. Under the yellow light of one, I manage to stop crying and dry my cheeks with my netball shirt.

'Howdja go?' Dad asks when I walk in the door.

'Good.'

'Good? Well, what position and who's in your team?'

'Same,' I say to the inside of the fridge. I don't tell him about the two divisions.

'Oh, that's good then, isn't it?'

When I don't answer and keep my head in the fridge, he says, 'Tea's in the oven. Amazing what you can do with one arm and leftovers! Ha.'

I lie in bed staring at Mum's picture. When I was little, we would walk down the hill together and I'd watch her play. Goalkeeper or goal defence. The ball flying in to the other team's goal. Her hand appearing and slapping it out to a teammate. After the game, we would walk back up to the town, my hand curled into hers. The long grass tickling against me. Now all that's gone. Mum. Netball. I'll tell Lizzy after the next practice that I can't play. Explain that I have to look after Dad.

At practice, I get scared with everyone around and can't tell Lizzy. I decide to wait till I can get her on her own.

She puts us in positions. This new girl Brooke, who looks like Pink, is in centre. I'm goal defence with another new girl called Han'a going keeper. Han'a's wearing track pants and a long-sleeved T-shirt under her netball uniform. The blackest hair I've ever seen down her back. A scarf covers her head.

We run up and down the court passing the ball to each other. Brooke throws bullets. I feel a finger go numb and the ball flies up and over the fence. Brooke laughs. Han'a doesn't seem to know what to do and can't catch Brooke's passes. The more we drop them, the harder she throws. She's trying to break our fingers.

After practice, we sit in the little tin shed at the side of the court for a team meeting. Lizzy says because there are eight of us, each player will have to sit out equally. Well, I won't be playing, so that fixes that. I open my mouth to speak but Lizzy looks at me, a finger to her lips.

'Listen,' she goes. Her long fingers touch the club's emblem on her netball shirt. 'The captain of this team has to be someone who knows what it is to play for each other. I've chosen Rachel.'

Me? I'm not even going to play. Why not super-girl Pink, the tallest and best player by far? Just ask her. Brooke glares daggers at me. She wants to be captain. Well, she can have it. And this stupid team.

I look up at Lizzie. 'Well, I'm not…'

'Han'a, you'll be vice captain.'

Han'a nearly falls off the wooden bench. She'd been hunched over, holding her bruised fingers. But now she looks up with big brown eyes. Her back goes straight.

'Now, Rach, take the team for sprints.' Lizzy chucks me a practice ball before I can tell her I'm quitting.

Han'a stands up. 'Come on,' she says. She reaches out a hand and pulls me up.

The girls trail us out of the shed.

'Let's all follow the shortie and the rag head,' Brooke says under her breath like you do when you really want people to hear.

Lizzy shoots out an arm and wrenches her back into the shed so hard she nearly falls.

When Brooke comes out, she walks over to us. 'I'm sorry,' she says to me, and then to Han'a. Her eyes are red, make-up melted.

'No worries,' goes Han'a.

'Oh. You're Australian?' says Brooke.

'Nah. I'm Swedish. What do you think?'

Our first game is against Bays. Icy drizzle claws its way across the court, and into our bones. The rain stops and we sweep the puddles off the court, but it's still wet and slippery. The Bays' attack players are bigger and rougher than Han'a and me. They wear out the goal ring with deadly shots. But I learn that Han'a is not scared of anything. She cops a massive shove and goes down on the asphalt with a slap. She lies there not moving, her black hair drowning in the remnants of a puddle. When I help her up, there's pain in her dark eyes. But then she flicks water out of her hair, reties her scarf and limps into position. The next attack, she jumps, arm soaring, fingers slapping the speeding ball out of space, straight into my hands. I whip it to Bec, who is darting up the wing. She shoots to Brooke, whose flat pass to our shooter splits their defence. Goal.

The Bay coach roars at his team from the sidelines. 'Move your bloody selves! Too slow! You idiots!'

How strange and horrible it sounds. Lizzy would never talk to us that way, and we're hopeless. Our supporters clap, except Dad, who can't, but I hear him yelling, 'Yiha!'

At half-time, we hear their coach ranting at them. Afterwards they come out angry. We're hipped and elbowed till my ribs scream. We lose by heaps but somehow afterwards the bruises are proud reminders of how hard we fought together. I think about the girls in the other team. They won, but to be treated like that by your coach is way worse than losing. I forget all about quitting.

The next game is away and we get thrashed. Then it's our first home game. Against Creek. Unbeatable legends of the league. Top against bottom. A few more parents come to watch. Dad picks at the plastic on his crook hand. When he thinks I'm too busy to see, he keeps sneaking over to the oval to see how the footy is going.

Lizzy takes me aside before the game. 'You decide and tell the rotations at the end of each quarter.'

Oh no. Telling players they have to come off is the pits. Everyone hates you. You have to be strong and not care what people think. I can't do that. That's not me.

Creek start like a machine. But they aren't rough, just good. Dad is looking over at the footy oval. When I fall, my opponent helps me up and apologises even though it wasn't her fault. Lizzy smiles and tells us we're going great. I sit myself out. In the second quarter, Brooke begins to pinch their centre breaks. Han'a works out her opponent and starts picking off attacks. At half-time, Creek leads by just two goals.

I feel bad telling Han'a she has to go off but she smiles and says, 'Good, I need a rest,' and skips off the court.

At three-quarter time, it's Brooke's turn to sit out. To make it worse, her mum, tall and beautiful, is standing next to her. Probably telling her how brilliant she is.

When I get to Brooke, I'm shaking inside. But she's already taking off her bib.

Her mum puts her hand on my shoulder. 'Brooke's sit-out?'

'Um. Sorry,' I look at my feet.

'That's fine, Rach. Good to see a team where everyone gets a go.'

We steal their next centre pass, and goal. Our supporters are standing up. Dad stops looking over at the footy. Han'a and I somehow keep a few of their attacks out and get some rebounds to our own goal. It's like they have flat feet and we have springs in ours. But in the last ten minutes, Creek start to play again. We lose. But strangely it doesn't feel like it.

The crowd claps. Creek give us three cheers and shake our hands. Lizzy reckons it's our best game ever. We're playing beautifully now, she says. She doesn't say anything about winning or losing, just playing.

And we do start winning some games. Maybe it's because the other teams are in shock. Dad says it's not that. He tells me it's because we play as a team. And we have a pretty good captain.

The last practice before the grand final. The president watches every move. Arms folded. Slips catcher eyes. Afterwards, she calls just our team to a special motivation meeting in the clubrooms. Parents sit along the sides of the long room on tables. Han'a's family are there next to Dad and Brooke's parents. Han'a's mum is wearing a long bronze-coloured dress and a matching scarf. Dad's plastic arm cover and bandages are gone. He's got dried mud on the knees of his overalls from a plumbing job.

We're the only team in the club to make a grandie. We sit on the beer carpet, arms around shoulders, looking up at the pacing figure of the president.

'To make the league grand final is a great feat,' she goes. 'You must win.' She glares at me. 'Creek has not lost a game all year and now we have to do it.'

I look at the cigarette burn in the carpet and think about Creek cheering us. How skilled and fair they are.

'Whatever it takes,' roars the president. 'Best players in best positions and don't bother with rotating players. Use your elbows. Get stuck into them. Just win!' Then she shoves her fist in the air. 'Finals or fair?'

'Finals.' It's a worn-out murmur.

The president puts her fingertips to her ear, shakes her head and says, 'Fair?'

'What about fair and finals?' I say. No one is supposed to hear but everyone turns and looks at me.

Then Han'a breaks the silence. 'Yeah, fair and finals.'

Dad starts clapping, and Lizzie and everyone else is yelling, 'Fair and finals!'

Afterwards, Dad and me walk up the hill to home, the long seed filled spring grass brushing us. I hold my outside hand over its tips. Like leaning out of a boat and feeling the water going past. Next to me, Dad reaches out his big repaired hand. I curl my other palm into it.

'We won't beat them, Dad.'

'So what? It'll be great fun.'

Together we go up over the lip of the hill and into the town just as the street lights begin to flicker on.

Where's Pluto?

It's the happiness of home time on a Friday afternoon. For the other kids, not for me. I don't belong anywhere any more. I squeeze through the school gate holding the cardboard box over my head so it doesn't get bumped. I'm very proud of my solar system model. Shouts and laughter sing across the oval and the playground, and out into the street. It's a wide street. The town is big because there's lots of space. The houses have yards like paddocks, and each one with a TV antenna sticking up high to get the signal from Adelaide. The school is spread out along a whole street even though there're not many kids there. Next to it Pioneers' Rest retirement home. That's where Dad reckons Grandad should be but he gets out of it by making out he can't hear Dad.

I've been at Mum's all week for the first time and now I'm going back to Dad's for the weekend. Mum and Dad aren't talking. I'm stuck in outer space between them. The farm was my home but Mum isn't there any more and Dad has gone weird. Grandad has changed too. He had a heart attack and nearly died and now he can't remember my name. Mum's new place in town has got her in it but it's strange too.

My backpack is lumpy with clothes and stuff. As I try to hold up the solar system, my backpack catches on the school gate latch and spins me and then I'm through, sandals scrunching on the gum nuts and broken twigs. Dad stares at me from the Toyota parked at the curb. He's been angry since Mum left. Like he could easy kill someone. He hates everyone and everything.

'What's that?' he growls as I slide the model onto the seat next to him. Mars bumps against Jupiter and Saturn wobbles.

'Solar system.'

'Oh yeah?' He turns the model, tilts it up to look inside.

Miss Hampton said we had to make our model from recycled stuff. Mum and her friend Hadi helped me. I found an old red plastic ball with dog teeth marks in it for Mars. For the other planets, Hadi and me used the white Styrofoam packing from Mum's new plasma TV. He helped me glue and carve it into spheres to make the big planets. We used fishing line to hang the planets from the roof of the box. Hadi found some tins of old paint in the storage shed at the servo where he works. His boss was glad to get rid of it. The background of my model is paint and stickers – the deep blue night sky with bright spots of stars.

Hadi is good at making stuff. He used to be an engineer where he comes from. He built bridges and things like that. But I would never tell Dad that Hadi helped me. The sound of Hadi's name sends him nuts. Miss Hampton says my solar system is great. After I made it, I was so happy I forgot Dad would hate it.

Dad pokes at Neptune with a finger as if he's looking for something. His eyes are scrunched up. There are dark rings under them. 'Where's Pluto?'

'Pluto's not a planet.'

'What? Who says?'

'Miss Hampton. She said we could put it in if we wanted but it's not really a planet any more. She said if we put it in and kept the scale right, Pluto would have to be in Port Lincoln.'

'Not a planet? What rubbish.' He reaches for the ignition key. He crunches through the gears, his staring eyes searching the streets as we roar around the block, past the church.

I like looking at the church with its big old pine trees and rose bushes. It's got gardens like the houses in town, as though people love it and care about it. On Sundays, the church garden is chockers with people all dressed up. They look like they want to be there. Dad says people shouldn't go to church if they don't want to, and he doesn't want to. He reckons too many people get religious because they think they have to, to keep themselves out of hell when they die, or so others think they're good people. Dad says all religion is a lie but Muslims are the worst.

Mum has gone all religious. She never used to go to church. She told me she goes to play the organ and sing. And because she's sad about what happened and is starting her new life.

On the side of the church is a sign made of curly metal that says Christ Almighty. They must have been listening to Dad when they thought that one up.

We drive past the servo and Dad's knuckles are white on the gear knob, his eyes staring at the parked cars. He nearly dislocates his neck as he swivels to watch a man coming out of the workshop. It's not Hadi.

'Where is that bastard? What are they up to?'

I don't answer.

'What are they up to? Having a good old time because you're with me? You know, Andy?'

'Dunno.'

We angle park outside the IGA, front tyres bouncing us off the kerb. The planets go crazy inside their box. Mum's car is nowhere to be seen and I hope that she's finished her shopping. Through the big IGA windows I can see silvery figures inside but none of them look like her. Dad also tries to see through the reflections in the shop windows. I put the model on my lap and stare into its painted sky, the planets set out in a line, little Mercury boiling next to the orange sun.

Dad says something and I feel the shifting of weight, the door slamming. I wish I'd put Pluto in now. Even if it's not a planet, it's still there, isn't it, alone at the edge of everything? Spinning in the dark. Dad's right. My solar system is rubbish made out of rubbish. I hate it. On the footpath there's a round green metal bin, but the hole in the top is too small for the model. Maybe if I put it on the ground and jump on it...

Dad storms out of the IGA with some bloody-looking meat in plastic, throws it on top of my model, bowing the cardboard sky inward and shaking up the planets again. Now we're going to back out and head straight for the farm. Please! But he crunches out of reverse, flicks at the wheel and we do a wild uey, skim the other curb and head back towards the little house where Hadi lives. Dad's got that angry stare and he won't let it go. Even though I don't go to church, I try to pray that we don't meet up with Hadi.

We idle past the house, Dad trying to look in the windows. The planets sway. Then we go past the house that Mum is renting. No cars are in the driveway. Dad grunts, guns the engine. Finally we're going and I start breathing again.

When we get to the farm, Grandad's standing at the front window watching us. He looks at me like he knows, but then, like always he raises his eyebrows and says, 'What's his name?'

'Andy, your grandson. Christ almighty, you're getting worse. I'm gonna ring up Pioneers' Rest again, get you booked in,' Dad sighs. 'The boy's home from school for the weekend. I'm going outside.'

Grandad is big. His left leg is a bit wobbly but the farmer's muscles in his shoulders and arms still burst out of his dark blue pyjama top. He's an old, balder version of what Dad used to be like. Funny and pretty smart. But two days after Mum moved out, he had a heart attack and they said his brain didn't get much oxygen for twelve minutes. Mum's fault for dumping us and running off with a terrorist, says Dad.

I was at school when Grandad had the heart attack. They told me Dad kept him alive till the ambulance arrived. Now Grandad's brain is cut off from anything that happened after 1974. Dad's worked that out by the things Grandad comes out with. Sometimes he talks like Dad is still three years old.

The bits before 1974 are pretty good, though. Grandad's always trying to fix stuff that's happened. And he's still a good shot with his walking stick.

'What's that?'

'Er, solar system. It's crap. I'm chucking it.'

'Gis a look then, Bill.'

Grandad peers inside the box; his bald spotty head could be a giant moon that eclipses everything. 'Hm.' He grunts and sniffs at the Styrofoam and paint.

I hope he won't remember Pluto, but he says, 'Where's Pluto?'

'Gonna put it in later. S'not finished yet.'

'Well, Pluto's not technically a planet. I've been telling NASA that ever since I got back from the moon landing.' Grandad lifts his head out of the solar system and waves at the mantelpiece. 'Put it up there. It should be up high when we look at it. How about we put a light in the sun? Show how the planets are all part of it. They're all connected, you know. That'll look good.'

Then he limps over to the window to check the scrub and paddocks that fill the view. 'I shot down seven hundred and eighty-six Zeroes in the attack on Darwin. Saved the town you know.'

A crow caws from the front garden.

Grandad lifts his cane, sights along it at the crow and pulls the trigger. 'Peow. Make that seven hundred and eighty-seven.'

Dad comes back in. He's holding the phone and his hands are shaking, his eyes as big as Jupiter. 'I'm going out. Coupla steaks there for you and the boy, Dad.'

'Right you are. Bill and me are leaving for the airfield at sun-up. Flying to Washington to meet with Nixon. Reckon we can get him to talk to Ho, sort this thing out.'

'Christ almighty, what are you on about? The Vietnam war finished bloody decades ago. I'm going out.'

Dad stalks to the shed, and the Toyota is soon roaring past the house, heading for town like he's on a mission. He does this a lot. After a while, he'll come home drunk and go to his room, slamming the door.

A spoggy skips onto the front fence outside the window.

'Peow. That's seven hundred and er, how many, Albert?' says Grandad.

Dad's taken up drinking since he found out Hadi doesn't drink. It's against his religion. Now Dad's pretty much always coming home drunk. The more he drinks, the more he reckons people like Hadi get hand-outs from the government while real Australians get nothing. But I know Hadi works hard at the servo and he doesn't seem to have much. He can't even afford to pay someone to fix his dented-up car. He spent hours after school helping me with my model. But like I said, I can't tell Dad any of that.

They made Dad go to a counsellor person. He told Dad to give up drinking. But Dad reckons the whole world is out to get him and that anyone who tries to tell him what to do is a bloody idiot. So he makes a point of doing the opposite.

When I fall asleep on the couch, Grandad forgets I'm not a baby and that his leg is buggered and tries to pick me up to carry me to bed. I loved it when Dad used to carry me to bed. Sometimes I'd make out I'd fallen asleep just to feel his big arms slide under me. Grandad feels the same now – his chest is hard as a board and he smells good like the farm. But he stumbles and bangs my head on the doorway.

'Oh, sorry, Frank,' he goes, blinking at me. 'We need to get some sleep, lad,' he says. 'We want to be at the airfield at sun-up. It's a long flight to America, you know.'

I lie awake in my little room and the house is quiet. Through the open window, I hear a car go past on the main road. Then the Toyota coming. Its engine is whining, the tyres tearing at gravel as it turns and I picture it swinging into the farm. Already I can smell dust and burnt diesel but all I can hear is a pounding inside my ribs. Then Dad's boots on the lino.

'Dad?' When I pad into the lounge, he's huge in the moon coming through the window.

He turns and I can see the rifle gripped tight in his fists. A distant siren starts up.

'Christ almighty! Andy. Get back to your room. Now!'

The siren gets louder and headlights brighter than stars brush the night. I can't move and Dad turns back to the window, lifts the rifle to his shoulder.

The local police car pulls up by the shed, keeping its distance. On telly, they always park out in the open and police crouch down around them so they can have a real shoot-out. But these local police are quiet. Dad swings the gun, poking the barrel out into the night. He doesn't shoot, though, just turns away from the window and looks across the room at me. I'm trying to think what he's thinking. Then I see it in his eyes. He's really scared.

On the mantelpiece, my model glows. The solar system looks really good now. After we had tea, Grandad helped me sticky tape a little keyring torch onto the sun. I cross the room and press myself into the floor at Dad's feet, wrap my arms around his big strong legs. I look up at the solar system on the mantelpiece. I can see now that the light would reach Pluto if I'd put it in. Dad looks down at me. His face is wet and pale. It's really still outside. Maybe everything will be all right like Mum says. Things might go back to the way they used to be.

Then there's the sound of another car coming. Footsteps and hushed voices. A car door sneaking shut.

Dad jerks his head at every tiny sound, waving the blue barrel of the rifle. 'I've got an eight-year-old kid in here!' he yells out the window. and quickly pulls his head back.

Something clatters and there's a grunt and Dad stabs the barrel out of the window again. I can feel his body shaking.

Dad slides down to sit next to me on the floor. His eyes are bloodshot and he stinks of stale beer and the pub. 'I'm sorry about this, Andy. I've done something stupid, stuffed everything up. Make us a cup of tea, will you? Then I'll go out and talk to the cops.'

I'm heading back to the lounge with Dad's cup of tea when I hear more cars crunching down the farm driveway.

A voice booms out. It's the senior constable from town. 'Listen, Jim,' he calls. 'There's no harm done. Hadi's just got bruising. He's not gonna lay charges. Come on, Jim. Put the gun down and come out. We'll sort it all out. Star Force are coming. There's no way out now, mate.'

Car doors open and close. Voices murmur. Suddenly squares

of dazzling light slap through the windows and onto the floor and walls. Dad holds his arm out, waving his palm at me, and I stop at the entrance to the lounge, hot cup of tea clattering in my hand. Dust hangs like stars in the slivers of brightness. Dad is craning forward trying to see into the glare coming through the gap in the curtains.

I hear a noise coming from the hallway that leads to the bedrooms. A tall figure in dark blue appears, lifting a walking cane to its shoulder, aiming at Dad. Dad's been staring at the glare coming through the window but when a floorboard creaks he swings the rifle around, blinking at the sudden change in light. The gun booms and Grandad drops. Behind Dad, the window shatters and a huge black figure leaps through, wrapping its arms around Dad and crashing him to the floor. The rifle clatters on the lino.

I drop the hot cup of tea, turn back into the kitchen. The laundry is off the other side of the kitchen and it's got an outside door. I race out the laundry door under the clothes line and into the pepper trees, thinking that on telly the cops always surround the house, so the baddies don't escape, and my skin prickles waiting for the bullet. But the night is dead quiet and I think for a second that I'm asleep and maybe I'm just dreaming all this, but then why am I running from the bright light and into the dark, and why is Grandad lying shot on the lounge room floor?

There's only moonlight on the other side of the line of pepper trees and I keep going into the black scrub with its broken-down machinery. The scrub is a parking place for old farm things. There are rusting steel ploughs and strippers from the horse days. The body of an old EJ Holden ute that Dad used to drive when he was a teenager. The old green Land Rover with four flat tyres and no glass in the windows. I nearly crash into it in the shadowy blackness amongst the trees. I lift myself through a window and scrunch down into the metal driver's seat. The Landy smells like old hay and I can feel where Grandad's hands have worn the steering wheel thin. He bought the Landy at a government sale years before I was born, said it was an older model of the one his unit used in the war. The real war that he was really in. I imagine what the Landy's seen. Soldiers. Battles. Years with Grandad on this farm. Till it started to get too old. Dad bought the Toyota and the Landy got parked in the scrub. Into its own Pioneers' Rest Retirement Home.

Grandad's got out of going to the retirement home anyway. He's going straight to the cemetery. I suppose the funeral will be at the Christ Almighty church. But I won't be going. You should only go to church if you want to and I don't want to.

They won't find me here. I'm far away and in the dark. I can hear voices. It's like they're talking now, not shouting, not angry or scared any more. Except for one, loud enough for me to make out the words. It's Dad.

'Where's Andy? Where's my boy? I'm so sorry. Let me find him, please. Where's Andy?'

Footsteps, crunching of twigs. I want them to leave me alone, leave me out of it, like Pluto. The passenger-side door creaks open. A spotty moon head above dark blue pyjamas.

Grandad grins at me and gets in. 'Nearly copped it there, Barry. But I saw the rifle come up and dropped quick smart. Felt the bullet go over me head. All that SAS training, you see. Turns out it was friendly fire any rate. Set to head for the airstrip already? Good lad.'

Catching a Ride

From the cliff top, Derek Ryder gazed down in wonder at the beautiful ocean. The metronomic waves caressing the shore below reminded him of the sublime photos in the surfing magazine that sat on the marble coffee table of his Adelaide penthouse. He was going to master this surfing game – just like he'd felt such mastery roaring past that kid with his thumb out.

The boy had been walking along the stony roadside with a surfboard under his arm. He probably lived in the salty little town a couple of clicks back. Derek smirked at the mental image of the dust cloud his big four-wheel drive had covered the kid in. He'd even sped up a little, enjoying the power of his new Range Rover.

Hiding his car keys under a front wheel well as he'd heard surfers did, Derek unhitched his virgin board from the racks. Clutching his new wetsuit and towel, he scrambled down the cliff path to the deserted beach.

Out to sea, sparkling ridges curled into bull-nosed verandas, their hearts lit translucent by the early morning sun. Shore ripple hummed his name onto the shallow reef. No one was out. He'd come early to avoid sharing the waves, as he'd read he should do.

As he paddled out, he was surprised by how cold the water was. It wasn't long and he was feeling slightly numb and, if he was honest with himself, worried. The relentless waves were pile drivers. Foam forced its way into the estuaries of his sinuses like wet cement. His neck had begun to ache from watching the ruthless surf before it pounded him. Several times, his board slipped away and he was pushed under.

He fought to think positively. Don't crash, crash through, that was the Derek Ryder philosophy – and he always crashed through, while others had to send their lives to the panel beater.

After an age, he was out there, out the back as he'd read it was called. The place far from shore where the waves began their swelling birth, where real surfers hang out. His head hurt. It felt like an ocean was sloshing around somewhere in there. He tried to sit up on his board, legs dangling over the sides, nonchalant as an old hand like the surfers in the glossy photos he'd studied. It was harder than he thought and he toppled into the water twice before managing to balance long enough to check his surroundings. Below the rising sun, the sandy cliff rose up from the indent of the cove as though a wedge had been taken out of a crumbly sponge cake. The cliff was so high he couldn't see his Range Rover or the flat land behind the coast. And all around him was the lullaby beauty of the ocean.

He turned to look out to sea. He saw something swell and build. A wave. His wave. The clean blue monster rose up, teetered and bent right in front of his gaping eyes. Falling onto his board, he turned the nose to the shore and began to paddle furiously. The back of the board was lifted by a great force, the nose shovelled downwards. Terror and excitement rushed through him. Then the board and its rider were driven like a stake into the stomach of the wave. Clamouring water tore at his face. A twisting force grabbed his ankles and tried to insert them in the back of his head.

Thrashing his arms, he tried to set up a meeting with the surface, but it was out to lunch and not taking calls. His head was pummelled, ears and eyes gorged with thunderous blackness. The leg rope threatened to tear his foot off and he pictured the board's pointy nose boomeranging into his head.

Clamping his mouth, he fought the urge to suck in. You are going to die, said the roaring in his ears. An inferno started in his lungs.

…there he was, a baby on his mother's knee… She squeezed his arm, pulled. Mummy! The world was lighter now…so tired…I'm going to sleep now, Mummy…

Mummy said, 'Take it easy, man, I gotcha.'

He reached out, striking air. Air! His mouth screamed open and he gulped lungfuls of the sweetest thing he'd ever tasted.

Vomit seared his mouth. The blissful grate of solidity on his bum seemed to further revive him. Then he was being dragged up onto warm sand by the arms and dropped.

The smooth face of the kid he'd passed on the road stared down at him. Green eyes blinked at him from beneath a haystack of dripping blond hair.

Derek tried to speak but his voice box wouldn't respond.

'How many fingers?' The kid held up two.

'Nnnn.' Derek sat up groaning as part of his spine readjusted itself against a nerve.

The pain felt good. Everything felt so fine when you were meant to be dead but somehow you weren't.

'V for Victory, kid.'

The kid picked up his board and strode to the water, leg rope looping behind.

Derek propped himself up, felt a spasm in his left ankle, spat salty bile from his mouth. Blue glare filled his eyes and he groaned to his feet and staggered over to his towel. He wiped his eyes, hung the towel over his aching head and looked out to sea. He found he was noticing things in stunning detail. Like the way the kid expertly pierced that little board through the surf and paddled his way out the back effortlessly, as if he had an outboard motor attached. Derek's lungs and head began to clear and he realised he liked the way the sun hurt his eyes with delicious heat.

The kid turned now, caught a rising wave and carved down the face of the shimmering sculpture, flicked up and down the face as if on wings. The water bore the slight figure towards the reef, but he turned at the last moment and spun back over the top out of sight.

The kid repeated this over and over, flawlessly. Derek sat on the sand and watched. Time passed unnoticed.

The sun was overhead and other surfers were arriving when the kid finally strode out of the water.

Jogging to meet him at the shore, Derek held out a hand. 'You're one helluva surfer.'

The kid ignored him, headed for the cliff path, board under arm.

'Hey,' Derek called, grabbing his own gear and running behind as the kid bent forward into the cliff climb. 'Could you teach me? I mean, I could pay. Pay you plenty. I owe you…'

The kid stopped, turned, and looked down at his pursuer.

'I can pay whatever price you want. Name it…' Derek pleaded.

'Well, it is school holidays. You really mean that? Anything?'

'Yes, absolutely. Anything. I really want to learn to surf.' What was he saying? This was no way to close a deal. Perhaps he had lost a few neurons out there in that oxygen depriving hell wave.

He started to follow the kid up the cliff path. Reaching the car park well before him, the kid disappeared.

A few moments later, he re-emerged at the top of the sloping cliff without his board. 'You've got a deal,' he called down to Derek. 'Meet you here at sunrise tomorrow.'

Derek struggled to the cliff top in time to see the kid's surfboard jutting out of a rear window of his Range Rover. Grinning at him from the driver's seat, the kid called out, 'I'll leave it at the edge of town, keys in the same place you left 'em.' Then he gunned the motor, showering Derek in dust and pinging him with gravel.

Derek turned back to the ocean, and for the first time in years his smile actually reached his eyes.

East West Tiger

The ride into town was downhill. This meant he had six kilometres of uphill to get home after work. But if he didn't think about the hell of going home, going in was awesome. He always tried to leave before Dad was up, which was easy given Dad's usual state. He could freewheel all the way, but he pedalled hard anyway. Sometimes you really want to get where you're going. Then you're drinking speed. You're a crushed spring being released.

The very air changed as soon as he turned out of the farm gate and onto the limestone main road. He started to hear and see beauty again. The birds all waking up squeaking like gates, roos in the paddocks not even noticing as he sailed past, the sun still down but its light merging with his bike's jiggling beam on the white road. Each pedal stroke rebuilding him. By the time he got to work, he could feel his heart, his body, tingling with strength.

He had his own keys to everything in the servo. To him, they were a treasured symbol that he was trusted and valued. Our acting manager, Aarav called him.

After parking his bike around the back and opening the office, he took the padlocks off the bowsers and flicked the big loop switch. The pumps clunked and started to hum. Then he opened up the shop, watching the glassy lights blaze their welcome to travellers on the east-west highway. Click switches, unlock, stride around the concrete forecourt checking the litre counter of each bowser then hold the big yellow logbook against his hip and slide the pen into the special slot for it in the East West Tiger shirt pocket and give it a pat, job done, all shipshape. He'd stand at the edge of the forecourt looking over the strip of dry grass that separated the servo from the highway. In the middle of it the granite-cairn Sai had built for her lost baby. Twenty flat pink stones, one for each week they said it had lived inside her.

He'd stand there, hands on hips, boots on concrete, blue East West Tiger shirt, with the Bengal Tiger logo. He liked to run his fingers over the embroidered orange and black cat sitting with its front paws crossed, calm and fearless. Below it, his name in swirling gold bumpy letters – Steven – not Dopey or Knucklehead or Useless. He could feel Sai forming his name meaningful and proud, the chatter of her sewing machine as she sat at one of the little brown dining room tables and sometimes he saw her wipe her eyes as he passed by out on the forecourt and sometimes she looked so peaceful. The tiger logo and his name were imperfect, and perfect. The company had three shirts like this; one for Aarav, Sai and him. Sai had stopped wearing hers when her belly had got too big. Twenty-five weeks now, they whispered, like they were praying or not wanting to jinx it, and the peaceful look growing.

Each shirt was blue cotton twill with a tiger slightly different, individual, not stamped out in a factory. He loved his shirt and the almost matching Yakka strides and Rossi boots he'd bought at Bird's, where Mum used to work. Old Bird smiling at him shopping for work gear with his own money.

'God bless, Stevie,' Bird had said, holding his hand for ages as if he was about to head off on a walk across the Simpson Desert. Then the old man giving him his money back – popping it into the plastic bag just as he turned to leave.

He washed and ironed his uniform himself at home. When home, look busy, or better still don't be home.

After everything was switched on, he liked to watch and wonder for a few minutes at the world passing through all this space. Everyone on a journey to somewhere they wanted to go. Or had to. A sunlit jet trail with the shiny blink of a plane load of people at its head. A road train carrying complicated mining machinery or a massive tractor bound for Western Australia, gigantic tyres lugged over the edges of the tray. A grey nomad house on wheels. He liked it when heads turned and they saw him, and he'd give an important nod of G'day, I'm the acting manager, got everything under control, if you need anything here I am. And sometimes they'd nod back or wave. And sometimes they stared straight ahead like nothing mattered but where they were going.

This morning, the first car that came in was a maroon Holden Commodore. Two adults, a teenage girl about his age in a bright lime tank top, and two little kids piled out. He'd seen them a few times before. They were all laughing and carrying on and the littlies started playing chasey around the forecourt.

'Top day, eh?' said the father as he started to fill up.

The mother and the teenage girl went into the shop. The little kids ran in after them, making a crowd. This freaked him out. He was only one pair of eyes and he'd been done by shoplifters just yesterday morning.

It had been a family in a metallic gold Land Cruiser, all wearing surf clothes with bright logo swirls, the mother taking her time over whether to use EFTPOS or some of the wad of cash he saw in her purse and going on about how far it was from anywhere out here the distances are amazing what is there to do and where do you turn off to see the whales at the Bight? Two tweens in matching Roxy jackets swaggered around the shop texting and giggling. Afterwards as they all got in the Land Cruiser, he had a bad feeling about why you'd be wearing jackets this time of year. When he checked the racks of lollies and chewies, some had been taken. He was ropeable. He ran out to the highway and gazed down it to the west in case they'd turned into the town or stopped at the granite Farmers' Monument but nothing. He'd not known what to do. Tell Aarav? Aarav would go, 'That is no good, Stevie, but not to worry.' But it would still be a shame job. Aarav might think he didn't have a handle on everything. Still, the right thing to do was fess up so when Aarav came in he'd thought, I'll tell him now, but he still hadn't.

Now this rowdy mob was in the shop. The girl stood at the rack of chips looking at the screen of her mobile and at him. She gave a little nod at him behind the counter, a look of How you goin? Seen you round. He tried his best acting manager's look of I'm watching you so don't even think about pinching anything. Turquoise light from her phone screen or maybe the sour cream and chives chip packets bathed her face and neck and he felt like one of the bowsers being switched on in the morning, clunking and humming.

'Have you got any hot food, Steven?' The mum said.

'Huh? No, sorry, I've just opened up.'

'No worries. Kids, you can have one ice cream each. It's getting hot out there.'

The little kids each got a Bubble O' Bill from the fridge. The girl didn't want anything and she went to the door, turned and caught his gaze before he could pretend not to be looking and smiled. His mouth opened and he forced it shut again, feeling dopey just like Dad said he was.

The bloke came in pulled out a credit card and pay waved everything. 'Thanks, Stevo,' he said.

'You're welcome, sir.' Stevie opened the counter flap and went out into the shop as the mum chased the little kids towards the door. He had a quick look at the lollies and chocolate bar display. It was hard to do in a hurry before they got away and without them noticing he was checking up on them. But everything was right as.

He strolled out onto the forecourt as they got in the Commodore and the girl wound down the back window. The tips of her fingers came up over the door sill and formed into a little wave. His arm came up and sort of moved in a stunned Thunderbirds way. As the car drove away, she stuck her head through the window, smiled and called out something, her dark hair wind splashing the maroon metal. He stood there trying to catch what she said, but the words got blown to bits before they reached him.

He went back inside and turned on the food equipment. He put on plastic gloves and stocked the bain marie with Chiko rolls and chips, and the warmer with pies, pasties and sausage rolls. He set up the coffee machine, the caramel tang of beans shining and rattling into the hopper and he thought, I can do all of this. I'm something here. And then, what did she say? What did she say?

A rumble came along the highway from the west. Two Harley Davidsons turned in. Stevie watched them through the windows. The riders took off black open-face helmets, shook and scratched their heads. One was a stocky young bloke with worked-out shoulders, dark stubble and the glare of someone who had been riding behind a road train full of cattle. The other had a browny grey beard and it was like they were the scowl gang.

The younger one came in and paid for their petrol with cash and grunts and a smell like they'd diverted into the pub on their way through town. As he was about to go out, he turned with his hand on the half opened door. 'Hey, pimples, yousell motorbikoil in this dump?'

'Yes, sir. The engine oils are there on your left. We have a full range.'

The bikie went over to the shelf. 'Which one's the best?'

'The Castrol Racing, fully synthetic. Costs a lot but anyway you don't need that quality for a Harley.'

The bloke held up the grey plastic bottle of Castrol Racing, his forehead crinkling, working out whether or not this kid had insulted him. 'Owma chisit?'

'Thirty for one litre.'

'Thirty? Fucksake. I only needa top up.'

The bloke kicked open the door, carrying the bottle. Stevie went out, touched the Bengal Tiger on his breast, tried to breathe the tremor from his throat, forced his acting manager legs to take him over to where the man was knelt at his engine, pouring in the oil. The older scowler sat on his Harley smoking a cigarette next to the NO SMOKING sign on the white-painted steel pylon.

'Sorry no smoking, sir,' Stevie said.

The bloke took another drag and stared right through him. Stevie felt his leg bones shrink into pathetic twigs.

The young bloke screwed his oil filler cap back on, stood up and shoved the bottle into Stevie's hand. It was light, empty.

'Let's get out of this shithole,' he said to his mate, slipped on his helmet and got on the Harley.

The older one ground his cigarette into the NO SMOKING sign and put on his helmet.

'Sir. The oil. Thirty dollars, please.'

'Fuckoff, pimples. I only usedabit.'

Their engines shouted around the forecourt and Stevie grabbed the leather jacket. 'You've got to pay!

The bikes were a rumble fading east by the time he picked himself up off the concrete, cheek stinging where the bloke's fist had connected.

'I'll knock your block off, dopey! Fucking useless pricks,' he yelled at the highway, using Dad's words. He'd worked hard not to turn into Dad but some things make you forget.

'Don't turn into your father, Stevie,' Mum had said.

He was going to tell her he wouldn't, sitting there holding her hand listening to the hum of some machine connected to her.

'You're a kind soft boy and you'll be a good man, Stevie. Stay kind but not too soft, okay?' she said.

After that, he couldn't speak with his insides all melted. Words and sentences all dopey and melted. And then it was too late. And here he was, useless, just like Dad said he was.

He went inside, sat on the stool behind the counter, put his palms on his thighs and felt the shiver subside, the bones grow back a bit. He wanted to be a good man but he wondered if he could postpone that a bit and get a gun. Those bikies might come back and he'd get the thirty dollars. Dad had three guns. He'd had nine before the Port Arthur massacre and John Howard made him give six of them up. 'That was before you were born, Stevie,' Mum had told him. Dad liked shooting things. Dad said he'd shoot that knucklehead John Howard if he ever saw him.

'Boo!'

He nearly fell off the stool.

Aarav pushed him on the shoulder. 'Ha ha, got you.'

Stevie shook his head. 'Don't do that, Aarav.'

'What happened to your face, Stevie?'

'I dunno. Yeah. No. A coupla bikies. They stole some oil. I tried to stop them.'

'For a second I thought your father… Sorry, Stevie. Perhaps we should not let you open on your own.'

Stevie realised his mistake. 'I'm fine,' he said. 'They only got a litre. Won't ever happen again. I'll pay for it.'

'I am not worried about a bit of oil, Stevie. Do you want to go home? I will run you home in the ute when Sai comes in.'

'I don't want to go home.'

'Well, actually I have some things to pick up so I might dash off for an hour.'

Aarav's hour was usually two or three. He and Sai had got the abandoned Golden Fleece going again from nothing and he was flat out trying to stop Sai doing too much this time. Which was fine with Stevie.

Aarav looked at his watch. 'Sai will be in later. I will be back soon too. You will be all right?'

'Easy as, Aarav.

'Where would we be without you, Stevie?'

When Sai came in through the back, he was sweeping up lines of limestone dust left by the wheels of a farmer's tray-top. She called and waved him to come inside. When he did, she reached out and touched his bruised cheek with the cool back of her fingers.

'Is your father hitting you again, Stevie? I shall telephone the policeman at once.'

'What? No!' But he couldn't tell her about the bikie. She would know how hopeless he was. A dopey useless knucklehead.

'You will tell me?'

Last weekend, he'd seen her stand in the doorway when a pissed local tried to slip out with a packet of chips he'd grabbed on his way to the door. In a flash, she was blocking the huge swaying figure. 'I shall telephone your mother,' she'd said firmly, shaming him, hands resting on her belly, her face with the same deadly calm expression as the tiger on Stevie's breast. The bloke had put the chips back and apologised.

'Yes, I'd tell you if it was that, Sai. But it wasn't.'

'Have you had anything to eat at all today? Breakfast?'

'Not hungry.'

She took his hand and towed him to one of the dining room tables. After a while, she brought him a huge sandwich with green bits sticking out of it and a cup of Assam tea.

'Do not move until you have finished,' she said. Then she went out, walked across the forecourt and stood by the granite cairn watching Aarav's old ute come down the highway from the town.

Aarav drove in, jumped out and didn't even shut the door. In his hands, he carried a shiny garden trowel and a big punnet of flower seedlings. He walked quickly across the forecourt to Sai, kneeled down and placed the flowers and trowel at the base of the cairn. Sai put out her hand and drew him up into her kiss.

That night, Stevie rode home with each heartbeat hammering at his cheekbone. The bike's tyres tremored on the limestone road and sweat sucked into his shirt. He'd wash it tonight. It would dry easy as and be ready to iron before Dad woke up.

There was still a glow in the west and he thought of the Commodore girl somewhere in that direction. He wondered what she'd called out to him. He'd ask her. He would. He'd be at the servo every day and when the summer school holidays were nearly finished, he'd say to Aarav and Sai, 'What if I work some nights after school and on the weekends? I'm sixteen now.'

And Aarav would argue about education and homework,

Sai would think for a moment and then she'd get it. 'Let us give that a go, if it doesn't interfere with schoolwork? I shall telephone your father.'

'No, I'll tell him,' he'd say.

And he wouldn't be lying, but he'd do it when Dad was too wasted to bash him. And he'd be here at the servo to acting manage when the baby was born. There'd be no need for another granite cairn. Flowers would bloom around the one of twenty stones at the edge of the highway. And one day the Commodore girl would come in again. People did. It was the only highway east west. When she did, he would unmelt the words in his guts and try to form at least one non-dopey sentence. Here it was possible.

He pedalled uphill into the trembling headlight on the white limestone road, a pearl rolling into a dark enclosing shell. He wasn't pedalling very hard. Sometimes you don't want to get where you have to go.

Stretching Time

We turn into the Adelaide Pre-release Centre visitors' car park.

Pen switches off the engine and reaches for her bag. 'Just a quick half a fag before we go in, Joe… I'll pop the boot.'

I step out onto crumbly asphalt beneath a sky fighting with the earth over which can punch out the most heat. After a three-day heatwave, a heavy steel overcast has come in so low the very atmosphere feels like internment. There is no liberating breeze. Peak hour bustles past on Grand Junction Road just beyond a border of skinny gums. The smell of the KFC we bought on the way emanates from the Mazda's boot and melds with fumes of exhaust and overheated asphalt.

Pen sucks briskly at her cigarette as we pack the hot food in one prison-approved clear plastic bag, the cold drink cans and my homemade Monte Carlo biscuits in another. She checks her watch. 'Let's go. Better to be a bit early than late.'

We walk to the entrance with a straggle of other plastic bag laden visitors – a teenager in a tight olive summer dress, blue swirl tattoo on her calf; a well-dressed older couple who look only at the ground directly in front of their feet; a young woman in pink jeans, bright yellow blouse, nose piercings and beacon-blonde hair.

I follow Pen through a sluggishly heavy steel gate, down a wire mesh enclosed tunnel and through a glass door into a room where two male officers corralled behind chest-high counters are seated looking intently at computer screens. The room is warm, crowded, hushed. Waiting. It reeks of takeaway, apprehension, anticipation. The clock on the wall indicates roughly 4.50 p.m. We left Pen's place in Happy Valley two hours ago.

The officer closest to us looks up at Pen, raises an eyebrow, nods, almost smiles. She steps forward, hands over her ID. He gives it back to her quickly and she motions me to present myself. I pass him my driver's licence. He engages in concentrated mouse moving and screen studying the way they do at airline check-in just long enough to make you think there's going to be a problem. Eventually he hands it back. His face is expressionless, his serious demeanour part of the uniform. Pen and I move back to the edge of the visitor crowd like penguins relegated to an uncomfortable perimeter.

Olive dress girl emerges from the flock and approaches the counter, bouncing on sandalled feet. 'Can I run across the road and get Hungry Jack's for Mum?'

He looks up from his screen, nods at the wall clock. 'You won't have enough time.'

She bounces. 'Can't I? Oh. Please? Just run and get it quick?'

'If you miss the start, we're not allowed to let you back in.'

The energy melts out of her and she disappears back into the crowd.

'Are we waiting for five o'clock?' I whisper to Pen but she doesn't answer and I wonder if talking is banned.

She told me there are a lot of bizarre rules here – rules for the sake of demonstrating control. Each one strictly enforced. Time is measured precisely. We wait. I watch the clock's red second hand orbiting. At 5 p.m. the second officer stands up and strides to an open area on the other side of a security-screening gate. Visitors shuffle, teeter at edges of authorisation, move forward. Silently they go through and he waves a black metal-detecting paddle over them, being particularly thorough with inside legs, groins and armpits.

'You should be able to do this with your eyes shut by now, Penny,' he says when it's our turn.

They both laugh, chat briefly, warmly, enjoying this shared repeated ritual. He barely checks her, but reinstates his stern silence to paddle scour me as if I'm Schapelle Corby.

I follow Pen through yet another glass door and into a large room of white plastic furniture. A few people are sitting talking. I try to differentiate prisoners and visitors but can't tell the difference. There seems to be no prescribed prisoner uniform, apart from a preponderance of plain T-shirts – khaki mostly, with the occasional black or stark white. We could be in a workplace cafeteria at break time – except there is no feeling of familiarity or belonging, no chortling banter. I know from what Pen has told us that amongst this mixture of visitors and low-security inmates are fine-defaulters and repeat drunk drivers. There are also paedophiles, rapists and murderers who have served lengthy sentences and are now being prepared to re-enter the world.

'When we're in there, don't ever talk about what someone's done,' Pen warned me on the long drive from the southern suburbs. 'It's an unwritten rule. They might be low-security but they're still locked up – they're obsessed with time, not crime. It makes some of them crazy. Did you hear about that woman? Never returned to the prison after work at some factory on the outside? She was eventually found in a motel room. She'd slashed her wrists and bled to death. All alone. Can you imagine?'

I don't know if I can. But what I can feel is how this tantalisingly adjacent freedom would get to you, mocking you and your mistakes. Freedom looms here. It is constantly audible and visible in the passing traffic, the rooves of suburbs lapping at the sky and fading into the purple lure of the Adelaide Hills. Andrew and the others get to taste it by being allocated a bed in a crowded little cottage with a real kitchen and bathroom, in a day job or community service outside, work on the prison farm or distribution centre.

'Let's go out there.' Pen nods at a glass door.

Faded non-lethal plastic chairs and tables slump under a sky so oppressively metallic it could have been created by the designers of Yatala Labour Prison – the forbidding nineteenth-century stone and wire complex we passed a little earlier on Grand Junction Road.

We sit on white chairs that have absorbed buttock-searing heat. Olive dress girl comes outside with an older woman, their arms around each other. Others drift out too, toting clear plastic bags of food and drinks, prisoners and visitors indistinguishable. Genders are permitted to mix with minimal supervision here – another taste of normality, humanity.

'Does he just come out, Pen?' I ask after a while of nothing happening.

'He can't leave his cottage until they call him officially. They said they've called him. You have to be patient in this place. Let's get our picnic ready.'

'But he knows we're here?'

'Yeah, but he can't come until he's called. Another one of those rules…'

We empty the plastic bags onto the table and arrange an approximation of an evening meal – KFC dinner box or whatever they call it for Andrew, Pen's wrap, my burger, drinks, and four huge biscuits in their plastic container – the one thing truly from home. I wanted to bring a stack of biscuits but they aren't allowed to take anything back to their cottages. 'Only bring enough that we can eat during visiting,' Pen had said when explaining the procedures to me over the phone.

She fishes through the KFC containers. 'Bummer. They've forgotten the plastic cutlery and serviettes.'

The food is screaming scents of greasy herbs and spices. We keep peering through the glass door, checking our watches.

'They said they called him,' Pen says.

A minute later, she pushes her chair back. 'I might just check.'

She comes back out. 'They're pretty sure they've called him… they're gonna see.'

We wait. I look at the golden biscuits with their pink homemade filling of fresh crushed strawberries, icing sugar and butter melting and the oil-stained red and white KFC boxes waiting and the cans of Pepsi and Mountain Dew sweating. Pen keeps glancing at a NO SMOKING sign as if she's hoping it will disappear, fidgets, fills the time by reminiscing about her last happy fishing trip with Andrew on Yorke Peninsula.

That was before his sentencing for engaging in a consensual relationship with a fifteen-year-old girl when he was in his early twenties. Over half his lifetime ago. She is now an adult with a family and wanted him charged. He immediately pleaded guilty, was, is, extremely remorseful and ashamed. But, despite an otherwise unblemished life, a loving stable family, and his victim stating that she didn't want him jailed, the judge gave him eighteen months. Pen thinks it's because he looks like a bikie. I think it might also be to do with rightful community disgust at the horrific paedophilia, sexual abuse and bad behaviour by men in power constantly coming to light. And Andrew looks intimidating. He's a stereotype of shovel-blade beard and muscle.

I try not to look at my watch for a whole minute; nor to stare at the food. Andrew asked specifically for KFC. He doesn't usually eat fast food, but here we are with it and I can understand his craving. It's a hunger for things he can't get in here. Last week, Pen brought him Vegemite sandwiches. Vegemite is banned inside because prisoners use it to make alcohol. But it's okay to consume in this low-security visitors' space. He'll be thoroughly searched before he goes back to his cottage.

The glass door shudders. A huge dark shape emerges like something coming out of a hibernation cave. Andrew. Plain black T-shirt, new-looking blue jeans, black sneakers. It's twenty-past five – twenty minutes of the precious allocated eighty gone. He spots us and strides over. Pen stands, reaching for him.

'Sorry. They didn't call me,' he says with a slump-shouldered shrug of what can you do?

They hold each other and I lean away, feeling beyond awkward. Embracing is allowed only at the beginning and end of each visit and they're making the most of it. I can hear them kissing and I wish I wasn't here trespassing on this time so hard to get – the long afternoon peak-hour drive, paperwork, bookings, checks, approvals, waiting. A bureaucratic ritual of hurdles designed to test commitment. Pen told me it's a lot better, though, than Mount Gambier. She did that eight hundred and seventy kilometre round trip every weekend for the year Andrew spent in prison there. Sometimes with family or friends, sometimes alone. My wife, Pen's sister, did the trip with her twice, came back shaken by the experience and Andrew's depressed state of mind. She brought back the story of how Andrew had to dodge being stabbed as feuding inmates attacked each other during assembling Chinese-made Australian flags for Australia Day. One had noticed that the plastic flag poles were sharp enough to be weaponised. A vicious fight ensued and hundreds of bloodstained flags had to be thrown out.

Mount Gambier was awful but the fortnight Andrew spent in Yatala immediately after his conviction left him terrified and traumatised. There, he told Pen, old hands forced him to stand watch at a cell door while an inmate vomited his methadone allowance into a bowl and sold it to another prisoner. Freedom may be close here but Yatala Labour Prison glowers just down the road.

'G'dayJoeG'day. Thanksforcomingmate, thanksforcoming.' Andrew shakes my hand. Despite his size, he never goes for the bone-crusher.

We sit down and start to talk. Or Andrew talks rapid-fire and we listen. Pen warned me of this – that he has to get everything out in the precisely allotted visiting time; all this pent-up stuff locked in here with him.

Now time is dense, pressured, hurtling. As he talks, he attacks the food like it's the first he's had for days – gnawing, smacking lips, licking fingers, periodically wiping forehead sweat with the stretched up bottom or sleeves of his T-shirt. Cascades of words out and food in. When he gets to the little plastic tub of mashed potato and gravy, he scoops it repeatedly with a big finger which he then sucks hungrily, providing brief punctuation for his non-stop narratives.

I haven't seen him since his sentencing over a year ago and am taken aback. Scars of his punishment lie on him clear as lash strokes. His face is astonishingly lined and tired, the beard moulting patchy and white, not thick salt and pepper. His voice, once unruffled and melodious, is edgy and tripping – like someone rushing a precious phone call in a bad signal area, fearful of suddenly being cut off. It's as if the old Andrew is trying to peer at us through a tiny barred window and we're glimpsing shadow.

He asks about their friend Ron, who has throat cancer, and Ron's wife El, and the extended Yorke Peninsula fishing trip that the two couples had planned for when he gets out in April. There might have to be a cancellation now but the concern is not the lost trip but about Ron and El and how things go arse-up for people. There are gradations of arse-up – here, Mount Gambier, Yatala, cancer. With uncharacteristic pessimism, Andrew says it's a death sentence for Ron but Pen assures him no, early days yet. Give it time.

'Gotplentyothat,' Andrew says and lets go a fraction of smile.

He works in the prison distribution centre and says that yesterday when they were waiting for a truck he sat down and started reading a book. In here where boredom is clearly part of the punishment, he's become a keen reader – with a newly discovered love for history. A supervisor told him off, said he needed to find something useful to do.

'Reading is a useful thing to do,' I say, raising my voice and making heads turn at other tables. 'I heard that the cheapest way to lower the prison population of a society is education.'

'That bloke doesn't care. Most of them are good, but to some we're…nothing. Not even…human beings.' He gaps these words with wedges of anger, at himself or the system.

He's consumed by guilt and shame, Pen says. Over his crime of course, but she reckons it's more about how he believes he has let people down. That he doesn't deserve forgiveness. In the early Mount Gambier days, he was on antidepressants. Part of that came from the constant terror of being sent back to Yatala. Men were sent there periodically, for no apparent reason other than to balance out numbers. Pen lifted him out of it by ensuring visitors every weekend without fail.

On the way here, Pen confessed her fear that we might not get the old Andrew back – that the prison experience has taken not only the time adjudged to pay for his crime, but deeply human parts of his personality.

I think of the books I brought for him that are out in the car and now probably smell like KFC. I'd arrived at Pen's early, having been warned that under no circumstances could we be late. Trying to be helpful, I'd already put them in her Mazda's boot before she told me we couldn't bring them in. She explained that prisoners have to apply for specific titles and clearance takes a week, or a month, or two, depending on when the prison authorities get around to it.

'Leave them there,' she'd said closing the boot. 'I'll get them to him.'

Andrew started his reading passion with some old thrillers she'd kept from before they met. Among them, incongruously, was an old Australian history book. That lit a flame. He declared he wanted to read history back as far as he could go and work his way forward from there. But when does time begin? He couldn't Google it, so she did and bought *A Brief History of Time*. After that, she couldn't get books to him fast enough. He reread many when clearance of new titles was stalled.

He has worked his way through deep time – the cosmos, dinosaurs, the arrival of humans on earth and so on. I figure he's pretty much up to my frontier histories of European settlement and indigenous dispossession in Australia. But that story will have to serve time too till all the procedures are followed correctly.

My burger is long gone. Andrew is wiping and re-wiping final atoms of mashed potato into his express-talking mouth and Pen is eating chips with incredible steadiness. I'm sweat-glued to the chair and staring at the four massively delicious biscuits in their container. I wish I'd brought more. I wait.

Eventually, Andrew peels the plastic lid off, takes out a biscuit. We follow his lead. Andrew's biscuit disappears in the time Pen and I have eaten a quarter of ours.

'Mmmmgood. You made these, Joe?'

'Yes, mate. The strawberries in the cream are from our garden. That one's yours too,' I say, nodding at the last biscuit.

'Geethey'resensational. Thanksmate.' There's a biscuit crumbed smile that sticks long enough to reach his eyes, and he shoves the last big chunk into his mouth as his other hand reaches into a pocket and unfolds a slip of paper. 'SoIdon'tforget.'

He flaps the paper apologetically. He'll have to wait another week before he sees Pen again. She said it's hell for him after a visit when he remembers something he wanted to say but didn't. He goes through the list – house gutters, sourcing an unusual paint colour for their panel-beating business, their daughter Courtney starting uni this year and her birthday party he'll miss out on – the marching on of normal life, all of which Pen has under control. Last on Andrew's list is that Pen is his 'Best fishing buddy ever. Just wanted to say that.' Each word hangs in the hot air, the meaning so indivisible and powerful they both stop talking.

The door cracks open and a uniform calls, 'Time!'

Chairs scrape, traffic hums, the grave sky yielding no blue. In this sweltering grey world, my eye is drawn to a snicker of colour shimmering behind the glass door and when someone opens it I see it's the pink jeans yellow top young woman. Now I understand her fine defiance.

People stand, hugging, whispering. Just people. Being together. All serving a sentence, incarcerated in separation and waiting. I step away and long to disappear but I can't so I look at the wire fence and the tops of cars going past on Grand Junction Road and beyond that the great undulating sea of suburban rooves. As they kiss and whisper, my heart is tearing – but what's it like for them? There are golden biscuit crumbs on the hot white table top and I brush at them with my palm like I'm suddenly in charge of cleaning up.

They break, arms stretching, holding every moment before he turns and enfolds me in damp arms.

'Thanks for…coming, mate. I really appreciate it. Thanks for coming. Thanks. Really appreciate it.'

'Thanks, er… See ya, Andrew. See ya soon, mate.'

We're the last to leave and the check in room is now empty apart from the two unsmiling officers inside their corral. As we approach the front glass door to the wire exit tunnel, we hear Andrew's voice and turn to see him about to go through a rear glass door. Presumably he's just been strip-searched for contraband Vegemite or books hidden in body cavities.

'See you, Pen. See you, Joe,' he calls over the heads of the officers seated at their screens. He's a boulder in an insistent torrent, shoulders and face twisted back towards us, not wanting to go in the direction of his compelled feet. 'Thank you for coming. Thank you for coming. Thank you for everything. Appreciate everything. Appreciate it.' Now he's enunciating clearly, each word measured, given space.

Then it hits me – why he repeats himself in this way at these ends of precious moments. Every syllable and pause adds a golden crumb of time with us. A lingering embrace of delicious word built contact; separated, elongated, stretching out to hold us to him. During the visit, each second was a speeding Ferrari, and now he will go through that door to time like a tired lone semi chugging up a mountain road smothered in its own cloud of windless dust. To books, his cottage, the distribution centre where the trick is to look busy, the world just there through impenetrable wire and glass, the cross-hatched gullies on his aged face scouring into canyons. And Pen and Courtney and the others – the anxious, the bouncing, the bringers of colour, the scared families and friends – they'll keep things together and wait and hang on.

'See you.' His voice is thick and weary.

'See you, Andrew. All the best, mate.'

'See you soon, love. See you, love.'

We call across the officers in their corral of uniformed seriousness with our cracking voices and Andrew slowly turns away like a well-trained dog, exits, and the room stretches and snaps with the blow of the closing door and his big form fading, fading behind that shivering glass, and steadfast Pen breathing, breathing, and moments passing slow as the hour hand on the wall clock.

When he's gone, the two officers are looking up from their screens at us. No words are needed – their eyes hold ours and I can see their human hearts in their faces.

The Best View in the District

Ebby opened the heavy steel gun cabinet door. Inside were two rifles on horizontal racks. With one of these, she would get her revenge, but which one? Behind her, Nonno sat on an old oil drum, a vacant expression on his face, his watery eyes staring at a spider-web-covered antique horse collar hanging on the shed wall. Nelson Mandela sat at his feet, tongue lolling, watching Ebby.

The cabinet door released motes of dust. It had not been opened since Nonna died and Nonno went into himself. Nonno was a collector rather than a shooter, but in his younger days he'd been a crack shot. When she was little, Ebby had seen Nonno drop a fox with a single head shot from one of these weapons. It was heading off with one of the hens in its mouth. By the time he got the rifle, the fox was so far away it was an ochre blur against green pasture. Not bad for the first immigrant mayor of the district.

Now which gun did Nonno use to shoot that fox? Ebby tried to remember. She lifted the sleekest-looking rifle from its rack. The one that looked most like the sniper rifles she'd seen in movies. She held it up and squinted through the telescopic sight, but saw only a blur of corrugated-iron shed wall. The thing was surprisingly heavy and hard to hold steady, and after a few moments she propped it against the shed wall. In a separate locked steel box under the workbench, she discovered neatly stacked plastic boxes of ammunition. It didn't take long to find which bullets slid easily into the breach of the rifle and she slicked four of them into the magazine. More than enough. Then she racked the rifle, and closed the cabinet door.

'Come on, Nonno,' she said. 'Let's go and make tea. Come on, Nelson.'

Later, with Dad and Nonno both asleep, Ebby went on to Google Earth and investigated the dirt track that ran behind Jowley's property. There was no image of the house. It was too new. The track was called Jowley Road, though. The land there had been owned by the Jowley family for generations. She checked again for Jowley's company website – but that had been deleted, probably when the you-know-what hit the global financial crisis fan. On satellite view, Ebby double-checked that Jowley Road was a no-througher that ended in a patch of scrub from which the hill sloped down to the sea. No traffic. Plenty of cover. All she had to do was shoot as straight as Nonno. Not tonight, she decided. Tomorrow, Friday night. He always eats at the sports club on Friday nights and when he comes home, I'll be waiting.

On Friday morning, Dad was shaking Ebby awake. 'He's gone again,' he said, the words racing out of him. 'Come on. Gis a hand.'

They drove slowly down the track towards the faint glow of the coming day, and on to the smooth bitumen of the town road. Dad was leaning forward, hands strangling the wheel, scanning left and right into the shadowy gloom of the roadside scrub.

'He can't have got far,' Ebby said. 'We'll find him between here and town like we did last time.'

'Hopefully he's just going to work again at the council chambers,' said Dad. 'Sometimes he seems to know more than the rest of us put together, then other times it's as if he's not even there.'

Soon they were past the first houses at the edge of town, and in the street lights saw a figure in the distance. The white-haired waif in pyjamas and slippers had just crossed Newland Bridge and was passing the high school. They pulled up beside him. Nonno grinned and hopped in as if nothing had happened.

Ebby had heard Jowley's new house was extravagant. And now even in the middle of this dark Friday night, she could clearly see that it was. Through the trees and across just fifty or so metres of moon-silvered paddock stood a pinkish rounded building, with a tall turret tacked onto the side facing the roadside scrub where Ebby was hiding. A castle rather than a house. Typical. Thinks he's bloody royalty.

Nelson Mandela, the ancient little bitser who'd been continuing his life's mission of pissing on every tree on the planet, turned and looked up at Ebby. If we're not going home, I'll continue my explorations close by, his expression said. When you're ninety-one in dog years, it becomes necessary to conserve energy for the things you must do. Like marking territory. Looking after his people. And his people had become very sad lately. Especially this once-happy girl who'd freed him from his concrete and steel barred cell at the shelter, and brought him to this paradise of tree trunks and wheels. She'd been a pup too back then. Back when everything was good.

Ebby stood there in the roadside scrub, analysing Jowley's faux castle. A curved white gravel driveway led through the paddock to a double garage. Fawn-coloured roller doors were closed. An external staircase swept around and up the curved pink wall of the house and led to the turret. Beyond the house, Ebby could see the lights of the town nestled in its picturesque gully, and the January straw paddocks rolling in waves to the dark sea.

'The best view in the district,' she said aloud.

Nelson lifted his nose from the roo droppings he'd been inspecting.

They'd been there for nearly two hours and it was past midnight. Nelson didn't mind. He'd emptied his bladder countless times and so now sat himself, ears pricked, by her feet. The castle was gloomy and silent but she knew Jowley had to come home some time. When he did, she would shoot him as he got out of his car to open the garage doors. Well, maybe not, but at least blow out a tyre of his expensive car to show him how hated he was. Put the wind up the bastard and make him leave his home as well. Let him know what it's like to be scared.

The sound of tyres on gravel startled her. She watched the lights of the vehicle breaking through the trees, heard it hesitate and turn from the road into the long driveway towards the castle. It was Jowley's gold Lexus SUV.

Ebby lifted the rifle to her shoulder and tried to steady it against the tree. But her body was shaking and as she peered through the telescopic sight she saw only a wavering blur of pink castle dancing in the cross hairs. Bright security lights snapped on and the Lexus filled her view. One of the garage roller doors began to slide up and she heard the hum of an electric motor. Shit! Of course he'd have remote-control garage doors! She tried to keep the cross hairs on the general area of the front tyre, her finger brushing the trigger. Then the vehicle crept forward and disappeared into the building, the door humming closed behind it.

She lifted her eye from the telescopic sight. Breathed again. It was over. Jowley would get away with all he'd done. Mum was dead. Killed by a stroke. Within a day of hearing the bank was going to take the farm. Stress was a contributing factor, the doc said. Yeah, stress caused by Jowley, Ebby had decided. Jowley had killed Mum. The farm where Ebby had grown up and wanted to live her whole life was lost too.

Nelson lifted his head and looked at her. We going or what?

Ebby took a last look at the castle. The security light had gone out and the place was lit only by moonlight again. A door in the curved pink wall opened and white light fell out. Jowley stood in the doorway, his head bowed. She hadn't noticed there was a door there. It was curved and coloured like the wall, as seamless as the investment schemes the prick had concocted. Jowley was a tall man with a bald head that shone like polished metal in the bright light. There was something in his hand. She adjusted the scope eyepiece and the view sharpened slightly. He lifted it to his mouth and she could see it was a bulbous glass of black wine. He stared across the paddock towards her and she pressed herself into the tree trunk. Jowley looked directly at her, wobbled a little, stepped out of the doorway and began to climb the curving stairway up to the castle's turret, stopping every couple of steps to steady himself. Each time he paused, he turned to look directly at her. It was if he was daring her, mocking her. She shivered, hoping it would be impossible for him to see her in the blackness of the bush where she'd hidden herself. She was filled with hatred for him, a rage that he was laughing at her and her family.

Ebby lifted the rifle, wedged it against the tree and, with a little more adjustment of the eyepiece, his face came so sharply into view it was as if he was only a metre away from her. As he got to the top of the turret, he turned to look at her again. The telescopic sight was a powerful one and she was able to keep it still enough now to see the lines on his face clearly. An old face in the cross hairs of the rifle.

The eyes blinked. Light-coloured eyes. Not mocking, she realised, but full of sadness and defeat. A silver glisten of wetness on his cheeks. Eyes with a view that she suddenly did not envy. He had his ridiculous newly built castle but what had he lost? More than her. The respect of people that he'd let down, whether by incompetence or trickery.

Jowley brought the glass to his lips and emptied it. He threw it outwards as if he was disgusted with it, and it tumbled, falling and flashing through the reflected light. Then he climbed onto the top of the railing around the turret, balanced on his feet, one hand clutching the railing, like a squatting monkey. It was clear that he was going to jump. Wobbling there, he looked directly at Ebby again.

'Don't, please don't!' she hissed.

Nelson looked up at her, felt the anguish emanating from her.

She willed Jowley to step down from the rail, to pull back from the edge. He reeled backwards, flung out a hand for balance and somehow half fell, half stepped down from the rail and onto the stairs. Staggering back down, he reached firm earth again and quickly disappeared through the door and into the castle.

Ebby lowered the heavy rifle. 'Come on, freedom fighter,' she whispered to Nelson.

They walked along the edge of Jowley Road. Maybe the tyres of Jowley's car had dodged a bullet, but so had she. Depleted of anger, heavy with the family tragedy that had carried her to the edge of doing something completely stupid and self-destructive, she trudged along the dirt road with the rifle at her side, ready to step into the trees if a car came along.

The white figure coming towards her looked like a ghost. It was walking very fast, bent over, a torch beam sweeping the road at its feet. Nelson bounded forward in greeting and the face lifted.

Nonno was wearing his pyjamas and a bright pair of white sandshoes. He reached out a hand, took the rifle. Then he shone the torchlight on the trigger housing, showing Ebby something. A crescent of blue metal was attached snugly behind the trigger. A trigger lock. No matter how much pressure Ebby might have applied to that trigger, it could not be fired.

Nonno shouldered the rifle like a digger on parade, passed the torch to Ebby, took her other hand, turned and led them home.

The Other Side

Like a fugitive, I slot my new Corolla into the narrow Small Car Only spot, the one free space in shimmering acres of chock-a-block shopping centre car park. I feel a small flash of unfamiliar satisfaction. I'd loved my red Commodore wagon and this is the first occasion I don't miss it. But I had to trade it in – after I'd had the ruined duco fixed. This conservative beige hatchback is nondescript and as yet unknown at home. It doesn't rate a glance there or in the cramped parking spots of suburban shopping centres far from home. I'd got the dealer to put on the darkest legal window tint too, so that I drive around like a Mafia functionary in the right sunglasses and the wrong suit.

After checking there is no one around that I recognise, I crab sideways through the gap to the back of the car and inspect the endless sweltering lattice of asphalt, metal and glass. A silver four-wheel drive creeps past with its radiator fan roaring, followed by other hopefuls searching for non-existent parks. I've donned my new very dark sunnies and a plain black cap but already the psycho morning sun is stabbing at a spot between my eyes. The bottle and a half of Cab Sav I drank last night is making itself felt. There was a time very recently when much more than a pint of beer or a glass of house red at the Eagles club after a game would leave me feeling seedy. Now I've crossed a line into drinking alone and hidden in my house, and steadily upping the dose. The drinking feels less futile than the union-provided counsellor's advice. I thought he was joking when he'd said, 'I suggest counting sheep, John. Imagine each one as a positive outcome leaping over to your side of the fence.' I stared at him, but then realised he was serious. I went home and took up drinking and losing count.

As I walk head-down shimmying between cars, I instinctively

check windows for Eagles for Premiers stickers, signifying home town cars whose drivers I'd like to avoid. A runnel of sweat forms in the middle of my back, my hidden eyes scanning fearfully like a shot-up pilot limping through enemy air space.

An epic walk later, the blue and cream behemoth of Toys R Us looms above blinding car rooves. Inside is crowded with shoppers but a lot cooler. I pocket my sunnies and begin the search for the section that has stuff for ten-year-old maniacs. Despite an abundance of time recently, I've yet to find a Christmas present for Fearless Andy. This place is my last hope.

Thinking of Andy is one of the few things that feel normal these days. I'm still an uncle and tomorrow afternoon I'll be over on the peninsula. I'll get to spend Christmas with people who believe my side of the story unconditionally.

I check aisles before going down them but see no one I recognise.

A grey-haired woman with a little boy grabbing at toy weapons on the shelves and saying repeatedly, 'Look, Nanna. Look at this. Nanna, look,' passes me.

The lady rolls her eyes and I roll back, a shared gesture connecting the community of the devoted footsore relative.

'Kids,' she says.

'Gotta love 'em,' I say before realising. 'I…'

'I know,' she says.

A couple of teenage girls rush past nearly knocking me into a gathering of *Star Wars* figures festooned with cardboard signs that say 'with bonus light sabre'.

A thin dreadlocked man stands in the middle of the aisle peering at a flat box he's half removed from a shelf. He looks like an unemployed druggie. 'Sorry, mate,' he says as he edges forward to let me through. 'Any ideas for an eight-year-old? Boy.'

'Computer game?' I go to move on, but he wants to keep the conversation going.

Other shoppers squeeze around us or take alternative routes.

'We're trying to get him out of the house. Something that doesn't involve pressing buttons or looking at a screen.'

I'm impressed. 'Surfboard? One of those new types, dense foam, can't hurt them much, fits inside most cars. Gave one to a nine-year-old last year. Loves it.'

The bloke looks at me as if I've just cured bad hair days forever. 'Thanks, man. I'll check it out. Hey, anything I can help you with?'

'Er, ten-year-old. Fearless. Surfs like a champion. Got all the surf gear already, though.'

'Skateboard? Got one, I s'pose?'

'Yeah.'

'Well, how about one of those plastic twisty things, rip sticks or whatever they're called? Look like a stick of liquorice that someone's driven over. My nephew's got one and he does amazing tricks on it.'

'OK, worth a look.'

The bloke waves a hand indicating possible directions. 'Good luck.'

'You too.'

I misjudged the man. Just a short conversation of shared helpfulness and I feel better. It's like I've stepped over a border into a country where people don't look at me as if I've tortured a family member to death. Driving all this way to avoid bumping into anyone I know is turning out okay. Now if I can just find the right present for Andy.

I squeeze past a pair of young mums comparing toys and labels sceptically. One is levering open the end of a brightly coloured box to see if the inside matches what is printed on the outside.

Eventually I find the skateboard-related shelves. They're stacked with a vast confusion of trucks, decks and skateboards that gloss and glow, calling new fearless skaters to the wind in hair busted knees experience. Where the heck are the rip sticks?

Behind me. Other side. Ripstik. A narrow tube connecting two flat bulbous ends. 'Surf on land!' the label shouts in bright exploding letters. Great. Now hit the checkout, Dan Murphy's for some wine and then back to the hideout/house, car in the shed, blinds drawn.

Got some left over wrapping paper. Tomorrow I'll be on the other side of the gulf checking out the surf with my brother and his family – including Fearless Andy. A chance to breathe and love and feel normal, not judged and presumed guilty.

I grab the elongated box and shimmy politely past people trolling or staring vacantly at mesmerising plastic. At the end of the aisle is a row of checkouts but only one is open and it has a line of people corralled in a twisting lane of barriers. Resignedly, I latch on. The old lady and the little boy pull in behind me. She's carrying a couple of small boxes and he's waving a silver plastic sword. I peer ahead and my heart sinks.

Manning, personing, the checkout is a girl from my last year twelve class. Ally. Scarily bright but a bit weird. A loner. One of the top students in my English class. Always wore as much black as she could get away with. Her single mum had drug issues, we were told, whatever that implies. No one ever showing up for parent-teacher interviews – unusual for a straight A student. She's an older more terrifying version of the year nine girl who'd stitched me up.

I shrink into myself, hiding in the line, vulnerable, powerless. These girls can wreck your day or the career you love. Especially ones like this with issues and melancholic dress sense. The year nine one eventually admitted that I might not have deliberately brushed her breast with my hand while checking her work. I'd kept her in for a few minutes because she'd been mucking around all lesson. At first, her complaint said this was a deliberate ploy to get her alone. But much later, during the investigation, when other students coming and going and just outside the windows saw nothing, she said she might have just been angry at me and the breast-brushing didn't happen or was an accident. But she waited till I'd been suspended and the school year was spluttering to a close, the department dragging its infamously leaden heels, the community with judgements already locked in.

No apology, no acknowledgement from the department that I'd been telling the truth all along, and the breast-brushing did not happen, even accidentally. 'Just stay home now it's nearly the end of the year,' they said, act as if nothing happened; while we sweep all the unsettled dust under the massive carpet we use to cover our arses.

I peek around the shoulders of the stout lad in front of me. Ally's blithely serving customers. What will she do? Abuse me in front of everyone, or refuse to serve me as had happened at my local shopping centre? I look at the Ripstik box. I'll put it back on the shelf and scarper. Drive somewhere further from home. As I begin to sidle out of the line, I spot Ally glancing at me as her hands work. Shit. If I go now, it'll shout GUILTY. If you're innocent, why did you run, the cops say on telly, usually after they've tasered some black guy. Don't they know fear can make you run faster than guilt? She passes a customer their receipt and the line shuffles forward.

Then I see that the exits are set up with one-way barriers so that customers have to go through the checkout whether they've bought something or not. I'm fenced in. Again she glances at me. The line swells and tightens like a ligature. The child's sword stabs me in the back. The throbbing between my eyes crosses over to my temples. I fumble sunglasses from my shirt pocket and hide eyes behind their feeble armour. Like a half-blind sheep in an abattoir, I inch forward.

Through the dark lenses, I watch Ally's long dextrous fingers work the scanner, lift and turn boxes, transact with swift amazing skill. Her skin is white as paper, her expressionless face sternly chiselled, contrasted by jet-black spiky hair and glinting wince-inducing multiple piercings. 'Emo lite,' one of the teachers had whispered disparagingly in my ear when she won the year eleven biology prize last year and stood stunned at the front of the assembly as if waiting for someone to say sorry, we've made a mistake. The bright aqua Toys R Us polo shirt she's wearing gives her an incongruous breath of colour.

The queue shimmies forward again. Three customers from confrontation. I wonder which side Ally took – if she was one of the students who signed the online petition supporting me, or one of those urging me to commit suicide. Did she put one of those anonymous cards of support in my letter box or a dog turd? Was she one of those drunks who came in the middle of a Saturday night and scratched PEDO in the bonnet of my Commodore?

Ally finishes serving a customer and as the line moves forward she turns and runs from her checkout. She sprints across the front of the store and disappears through a white STAFF ONLY door.

'What the heck?' calls someone.

'Hopefully she's gone to get someone to open another checkout,' says someone else.

'Bloody hope so. Fancy having only one checkout open at Christmas.'

No, she's gone to get someone else to serve me, or something nasty to throw in my face. The STAFF ONLY door opens and Ally races back and into her checkout cubicle.

'Sorry everyone,' she announces. 'Had to get something.'

A huge guy behind the old lady says, 'Get more bloody staff would be good.'

Ally looks at her watch. 'Sorry. Someone else will be here in a minute.' She keeps serving with calm rapidity as if her sudden brief dash was imagined.

Soon I'm in front of her. 'Hi, Ally.' I say as confidently as possible and hand her the Ripstik, steeling myself.

'Hi, Mr Davis. Taking up skating?' Sarcasm, pierced eyebrow raised.

'Er, no it's for my ten-year-old niece.'

Ally examines the box. Black fingernails and the flash of a tattoo on the underside of her wrist. A hint of barbed wire or maybe a snake poised to strike. Typical. She's taking her time now, not slick and super fast as with other customers. Selecting the right words to shame me. Dog turd on its way.

'Come on,' hisses the big guy in the line.

A bald man in a purple store polo appears, arms waving, putting a palm out at an imaginary spot in the line somewhere behind me. 'Opening up checkout two, shoppers. This way please. Sorry for the delay.'

The big man says, 'About bloody time,' and lumbers away with surprising speed.

The line depletes, pressure drops as people calculate and try to choose the potentially speediest line.

Ally scans the bar code, checks the box again, pretends to study the screen while removing a half-size credit card from her pocket.

'Why didn't you come into school to see us?'

'I wasn't allowed to enter the school grounds. To be exact, I wasn't permitted within two hundred metres of the school boundaries or any student. No emails or any contact or communication allowed. Luckily you year twelves had all but finished.'

'That sucks. We really missed you.'

'Really? A lot of people didn't.'

'Not a lot. A few. Not anyone who knew you or been taught by you.'

'Thanks, Ally. Where did you go just before? When you ran out in such a hurry?'

She scans the small card and the price on the screen drops by a few dollars. She holds it up pinched between thumb and index finger. 'To get this. Staff card. So I could give you a discount on the Ripstik. Sorry, it's not much.'

I can see the small tattoo on the underside of her wrist now. It's the barbed wire wrapped candle of Amnesty International.

She hands me the box.

'Ally, I… Thanks. Means a lot.'

'Will you go back? Teach again at the school?'

'Don't think I can face it. It'll never be the same, I think.'

'You should. You know she moved to Melbourne?'

'Who?'

'That year nine girl. I heard she's bragging on Facebook that she knows how to get rid of a teacher.'

I feel a sharp prod in my back again and glance around apologetically. The nanna puts her hand on her sword waving grandchild's head and smiles as if to say, 'This is the most interesting conversation I'm likely to hear today, so please carry on.'

'And you, Ally? What are you hoping to do now you've finished?'

'Medicine, I hope. If I get the ATAR.'

'You will.'

'I'm worried about the interview, though. Do you think I should take these out for it?' She taps her nose ring with the tip of a glossy black fingernail. Her nostril quivers. 'Change my hair, show them my conservative side?'

'Probably a good idea,' says the nanna warmly.

'Yes. Probably, a bit,' I say. 'Till you get in at least.'

The line twists and murmurs, refilling. I move forward under its peristalsis, taking the receipt from her hand, the flash of her Amnesty tattoo reminding me about prejudging.

'Good luck, Ally.'

'You too, Mr Davis.'

I move through the sensor barriers and the automatic doors shuck open. I glance back and Ally smiles before turning to serve the old lady. I lift my chin and step out into the heat.

Snack Empathy

'I'm off, Jas,' I called from the hallway.

'Okay, drive carefully,' came my wife's muffled reply from the bathroom. Lately she's been showering with the door closed.

Jas has struggled with her weight in recent years and become quite self-conscious about it. 'I need help,' she'd said when she told me about her latest diet, her defeated tone and slumped shoulders silencing my rabid cynicism about the rip-off weight loss scams she gets sucked in to.

It's hard for us older folk, I know. I've put on a couple of kilos too in the eight months since I retired. But I can knock the weight off easily with a bit of self-control. I don't need any help. I make an effort to get out on my bike, and I play lots of golf. But Jas hates physical exercise. She said she gets enough at the hospital and can't see the point of riding somewhere you don't need to go, or chasing a little white ball. I realised then she'd never understand. All she wants to do is nurse, cook, and read. And lose weight. Come on Jas, I kept telling her, it's just willpower.

'I'll call in at the supermarket on the way home,' I called again.

'I don't want anything, Russell.'

The late August sun was out, making the afternoon drive to the office quite pleasant, particularly since I could now get there any time and there would be no staying late or spending hours on the phone at home. I had to admit, though, that I was missing my successful real estate sales career like a limb had been torn off. I'd been brilliant at it. I have this knack of knowing what people are thinking, beyond the actual words coming out of their mouths. I understood what buyers and sellers wanted, what was best for them, before they did. But it took its toll. Working twelve-plus hours a day (fourteen on Saturdays – I count golf and hanging out at the club as vital work-related networking) including running around to numerous weekend open inspections and auctions for forty-two years. I retired because I wanted some me-time while I was still in great shape physically and mentally. Even so, having no one call or need me was more of a shock to the system than I'd expected. Cycling and golf nowhere near filled the void.

So last week I talked to my business partner Kevin (I still own a ten per cent interest in the franchise, so partner isn't stretching things) about volunteering to mentor both him and the sales staff. Lisa Metcalf, for example. The poor dear is roughly the same age as Kevin – early fifties – but just beginning her real estate career. In contrast, Kevin had been my most senior sales consultant and I'd sold him ninety per cent of the business. Lisa was a burnt-out ex high school principal looking for a life change. Kevin took her on to help fill the massive void created by my retirement. I'd met Lisa when I'd popped in to talk to him about my idea.

I remembered that chat well. Kevin had seemed hesitant at first, rearranging papers on his desk and looking at his phone. I assured him he didn't have to pay me. Christ knows, I don't need the money. I was glad to give something back.

'One afternoon a week?' he'd said, his stern greying moustache and steady gaze hiding his concern for me. But, like I said, I can read between the lines. I could tell he knew he'd be mad not to make the most of my wisdom and experience.

'If it goes well and I find I can fit it in around all my other commitments, I could do more,' I said. 'Attend open inspections or some auctions to show the staff the tricks of the trade?'

He'd smiled then, standing up and putting out his hand to shake mine. 'No, that's beaut, Russell. A couple of hours – but once a month would be sufficient at this stage. We don't want to impose on your retirement.'

Now as I steered my BMW into the office car park, I thought it strange that Kevin's white Toyota Camry wasn't in my old prime spot next to the staff entrance. This was taken by a gauche bright red Mini. Had Kevin sold his Camry and bought a girl's car? I doubted it. I had to park quite a distance away, and then walk around to the front entrance, as I no longer had a staff key to the back door. What a bloody pain.

There was a new receptionist smiling at me when I breezed in. She stopped clacking away on her keyboard immediately, smiled and made good eye contact. Kevin had trained her well. She was very pretty. Trim, lovely breasts, a particularly fine amount of excellent cleavage. Another tick, Kevin.

'Good afternoon, sir,' she said sweetly. 'Can I help you?'

'Yes. I'm Russell. I used to, er…? Kevin didn't mention I was coming in?'

'No, I'm sorry. He's out with a client at the moment. Can I get you a coffee or anything, Russell?'

Nice one, girl – use the person's name in your reply to help you remember it.

I gave her my best grandfatherly smile. 'No thanks, love. Any of the other staff in?'

'They're all with clients just now.' She looked at her computer screen. 'Let's see. Um, Lisa Metcalf might be free. Shall I buzz her?' She leaned forward and I had to concentrate on looking at her face.

'Sure, sweetheart. I've got time. And your name is?'

'Minnie.'

Sounds like that silly girly car out there in my parking spot, I felt like saying.

A moment later, Lisa strode, yes strode, from the back office area, and put out her hand. Her grip and smile were firm and all business. She was even dressed that way. Minimum make-up, buttoned-up blouse and dark blue suit jacket. I made a mental note to point out to her that a bit of red lipstick and cleavage helps close a deal with male clients, and women sales people should use this advantage. At the moment, she looked more like a school principal than a successful real estate agent.

'Er, Russell? Good to see you again,' she said, but her raised eyebrows said what are you doing here?

I explained that Kevin wanted me to come in as a mentor, and I was happy to give her a hand.

She glanced at the receptionist and then back at me. 'Oh? That's very kind, Russell, but I've got a few urgent calls to make. Er, you could help me out by looking at a property I've just put on our books. There's a good pre-market offer, and my descriptor might need some work. I'm still learning the ropes, as you may know.'

'Well,' I said, 'I'm more of a people person, but I'll have a look.'

'Come through.'

It was surprising to see that Lisa had been given my office. I felt a stab of covetous resentment as I glanced in and saw the familiar view of the little garden bed at the side of the building and my desk with its lovely dark leather top. Oh, the deals and commissions I'd made sitting there. Surely Kevin or one of the incumbents would have taken my office, as it's slightly larger than the others. I guess they think it's a hassle moving just for an extra couple of square metres. Still, I would have done it. It's a matter of seniority, of a real leader's place in the team. Like the car parking spot.

The next surprise was that rather than let me sit in one of the plush client chairs at the little round meeting table in her office, Lisa grabbed some papers and ushered me into the conference room. She put the documents on the long oval table and pointed at a photo paper-clipped to the front page.

'I secured this listing yesterday. Lovely family. The husband's company is moving their head office to Melbourne and it's a company-owned house – so they're selling. It hasn't been formally advertised yet. And I already have a potential buyer on the books – a young couple.' She brightened at this point, the matter of fact tone softer.

Give her a tick, I thought. It's important to appear interested in the welfare of ordinary people.

'Jake and Melina,' she said.

'Who?'

'The buyers. She's an occupational therapist, works with people suffering from MS, and he works at the botanic gardens. This will be their first home and they've been saving their deposit for years. I've shown them quite a few properties but they always just miss out. I really want to help them. The price is a stretch for them, but their offer is very good. The house is perfect too – not a fashionable suburb yet, but close to their parents, and enough room for the children they're planning once they get settled in their own home. And potential capital growth if the area takes off. It could set them up.'

'Interesting as all that is, you've got to remember, Lisa, don't get emotionally invested, especially in a first home buyer. Especially if they're a bit desperate. So can they come up with more money?'

'Oh. Well, no, probably not. But they don't need to. The vendor's not too fussed about price, as long as it's within market valuation, and their offer is.' She stepped back slightly, as if wanting to leave me with the papers. 'I'm not sure what to do…if we formally go to market, it adds a lot of costs for the vendor anyway…'

Excellent. This was right up my alley. 'You start putting the pressure on, of course, or better still find other buyers. Get some competition for the property happening. And we can make some money from marketing too. Remember that. Ditch the first home buyers and put your energy into cashed-up investors. With negative gearing, some of them don't mind paying more because of what they save on tax. That's what's driving the market, you know.'

'Investors? But what about young home buyers? What will they do? Rent from investors for the rest of their lives?' She looked at her watch. 'Sorry, er, Russell, but I've got to get back to work. Just have a look if you like. I'll see you in, say, twenty minutes?'

'No problem.'

'Help yourself to coffee and bikkies. You know where everything is?'

'Sure do, love.'

Then she went out and closed the door on me. Left me alone with a few sheets of paper and an almost empty glass water jug at the head of the table as if it was running a meeting.

I sat down and read her descriptor of the property. It was terrible. Way too factual. A student report rather than a sales pitch. There were a few photos but I didn't need to see the property to find the right words. I got out my pen and made some changes.

'The large windows in the lounge face the best views' to 'SUPERB interiors and PANORAMIC glass incorporate perfectly GLORIOUS views.'

'The living room has ample space for a dining table and looks out onto a pleasant outdoor area' to 'The GENEROUS light-filled living room and integrated SPACIOUS patio is an entertainer's delight that will be the envy of your guests.'

'There are three bedrooms; the master with an en suite' to 'the three HUGE bedrooms will accommodate any family with room to spare. The GORGEOUS master bedroom with its GLEAMING EN SUITE will deligh…'

And so on…

Soon I'd added thousands, at least, to the value. Once my gems of description were posted, cashed-up buyers or tax-avoiding investors rather than the young strugglers Lisa had on her books would be ringing her phone off the hook. I resisted the urge to knock on my… her office door. I went into the kitchen and made a long black with the machine. I looked at the biscuit jar full of Tim Tams, Delta Creams and Kingstons. Jas wouldn't be able to resist but I could, if I wanted to. Nevertheless, I took a handful with my coffee back into the conference room. No big deal. Just a ride on the bike tomorrow to burn off the calories. The bikkies were delicious and I made a mental note to pop across the street to the supermarket later and buy a packet of Tim Tams and a block of Snack chocolate. Jas had been very down lately and it would cheer her up. I often bought her a treat on my way home from work, or these days from golf or a ride.

Sometimes when she was on one of her stupid diets and we were watching television, I'd sense how hungry she was and bring out the family block of Cadbury Snack I'd hidden away. Her favourite. At first she'd say no but when I started eating it right next to her, particularly if we were watching a dessert challenge on *Masterchef*, she'd end up tearing rows of it out of my hand and devouring them. It was good to see her mood brighten for that hour or so, and we'd share a laugh at George or Matt's latest fashion catastrophe.

I had a look at the written offer from the young couple. Very fair, but that wasn't the point. There was no thrill in accepting a good offer when you could hunt for an amazing one. We could achieve more with some clever marketing and manipulation. They would have to come up a bit or bloody miss out. My bike had cost eight thousand, for Christ's sake. That sort of money was nothing. Lisa should be able to get much stronger offers with me in her corner. Forget the first home buyers and bait some bigger fish was going to be my recommendation.

Through the window, I saw Kevin's Toyota Camry come into the car park, hesitate and then nose into the space next to my BMW. Now he knew I was here, I'd get something really interesting and useful to do. I sat back and waited for him to come in and pick my brains. No doubt he'd insist I come in more often.

A phone trilled somewhere. I heard the staff entrance door open and close. I waited. I looked at my watch. Forty minutes since Lisa had left me in here. I picked up the paperwork and went out into the corridor. Kevin's door was shut and so was Lisa's. I knocked on Kevin's. Waited. Knocked again.

'Come in,' he called. He looked up from a wad of papers. 'Oh, Russell. Sorry. I forgot. Really busy these last months. Even through winter. We seem to be going from strength to strength. Do you want a coffee? I'd make one for you but I just haven't got time to scratch myself and, well, you know how to work the machine, or Minnie could…' The phone rang. 'Sorry,' he mouthed and put up a hand, and answered it.

I closed his door gently behind me and knocked on Lisa's.

She ran a finger over her eyes and looked up from her laptop screen. 'Oh, Russell. How did you get on?'

'Absolutely brilliant. You'll be pleased. I think if you incorporate my words into your web ad, you'll get wealthy buyers falling all over that place. Have a look.'

She spent a few moments scanning the papers looking more and more like a school principal who'd caught a boy wearing the wrong pants. 'Okay,' she said. 'Do you think that wording is accurate, though? The en suite is tiny, for example, and dated, and the living room is actually rather dark.'

'Ha. It depends on the point of view, love. If you see them that way, so will buyers. Accentuate every positive. That's how you sell.'

'Really? Even if you stretch the truth?'

'Lisa, seriously. You're never going to get anywhere like that. To be honest, you sound a bit like Kevin. I spent half my time rescuing deals for him.'

She stood up. 'Look, I've got to go to a showing. Sorry, Russell. I don't mean to be rude. You know how busy it can get in this business.'

'That's fine,' I said. 'I'll come with you and give you a hand. Is it to the house you had me look at?'

'Er, it's… Melina and Jake are meeting me there.'

'Who?'

'The first home buyers I told you about. They're very keen and want to bring their parents through.' She picked up a briefcase, opened it and began sliding papers inside as if she was annoyed at them.

Well, I was here to rescue her. 'Kevin wouldn't mind. He wanted me to help out, pass on my experience.'

'I understand. But, look, I just actually want to do this one on my own. Okay?'

'Oh? Oh well. Sure, love.'

And then she was guiding me out the door and disappearing down the corridor like Makybe Diva on the home straight of the Melbourne

Cup. 'Don't forget the income from sweetheart advertising deals if you formally go to market,' I called after her. 'I could mention the property to some guys I play golf with…'

Bill Davis came out of his office and I almost hugged him. 'Hey, Bill, mate! You old rogue,' I laughed.

He stopped and looked at me as if he was short sighted all of a sudden.

'Russell? What are you doing here?'

'Ah, you know, can't keep away from the place. Didn't Kevin tell you I was coming in?'

'No. Look, I can't chat. Sorry.' He waved an iPad at me and went to squeeze past but I stood in the way.

'Anything I can help with?'

'No. Not really. We'll catch up sometime. Yeah?' He spun past me and out into the reception area.

The corridor was empty. So was the conference room. Through its door I could see out the window to the car park. A small blue Hyundai with Lisa Metcalfe at the wheel looking straight ahead went past and turned onto the street.

A nauseating feeling of irrelevance came over me as I stood there blocking the corridor. I understood. I could read between the lines – another one of my many well honed skills. I could tell I was as much use here as that almost empty water jug sitting about where I used to command attention at the head of the conference room table. Out in the car park, my big black BMW looked out of place too, though I noted my perfect parking – unlike the red Mini which was at a slight angle. A phone shrilled and stopped. A printer or photocopier hummed and shhhd important pages through itself. People were talking in an office somewhere. The sounds of a world that no longer needs you are incredibly annoying. Well, at least I had my cycling and golf. Oh, and Jas.

As I drove home with the plastic supermarket bag on the passenger seat, I munched on the Delta Creams I'd taken from the office kitchen on my way out and thought of poor starving Jas. I wondered what she would be cooking tonight. She'd be really hungry after the awful overpriced shakes and tiny protein bar the new diet allowed her during the day. She'd probably insist on making steamed vegetables and some kind of unsauced baked chicken or fish.

I glanced at the shopping bag and smiled. Work might not need my wisdom and foresight any more, but Jas did. I thought of us watching *Masterchef* together later this evening. She'd be absolutely over the moon when I brought out the Snack family block and the Tim Tams.

Honey Trap

Leon tentatively towed his brand-new suitcase through the alien environment of the Adelaide international terminal. A pot-bellied man in a Led Zeppelin T-shirt banged a luggage laden trolley into his shins. The man glared at him as if it was Leon's fault and Leon apologised, though he had no idea what he'd done wrong. Wincing, he tried to follow the information on glowing signs and screens, the blaring announcements of urgent yet mostly incoherent messages, and a circular route of uncertain turns and one incorrect escalator.

Eventually, he found himself checked in and sitting in a crowded glass-walled space with a massive Vietnamese Airlines jumbo outside the window. The biggest plane he'd ever flown in had been a twelve-seater Regional Express turbo prop that had felt like sitting inside a metal coffin.

He blinked his sandpaper eyes and checked the budget smart phone he'd forced himself to buy for the trip. The phone shop lad had helped him download a free messaging app. His heart leapt. There was another text from Alena:

> In few hours I will meet you at Hanoi airport and we be togeter. I only dream of cudling al day and making love to my beauful Lion all nite.

Leon smiled. Even her misspellings, her Russian typos were beautiful. Immediately, he sent a reply:

> Soon my honey. Forever together. About to get on plane.

A petite hostess greeted him at the door of the jumbo as if she knew him and for a brief moment he thought this international flying thing was going to be good – until he squeezed into the tiny seat allocated him between a skinny black-suited Asian man and a hefty Australian lady who coughed wetly in his right ear the moment he sat down. He reluctantly followed the order to switch his phone to flight mode and wondered how humans were supposed to survive this for eleven hours.

Leon was not used to people, multidirectional noise, enclosed spaces that cut him off from the world. Eight thousand four hundred and fifty acres of prime farmland and no one but him had been his world for thirty years. And he was still in shock at the cost of everything related to airline travel. The long-term parking fees where he'd left his elderly four-wheel drive were surely a crime. As he'd stood there reading the sign listing the obscene parking charges, his fiercely austere father's refrain had come to him:– 'At least Ned Kelly was decent enough to have a gun and a horse.'

A long time after the delight of take-off, the thrill of jet acceleration, the synthetic meal, he fell into a fitful sleep.

When he woke to the lights and bumps of breakfast, his mouth was gluey. He guzzled the plastic thimble of water and tepid coffee and ate the tasteless food, trying to politely shield it from intruding coughs and wayward elbows. It took another unbearable age of lining up for the cramped toilet and then trying to find something interesting on the fingerprint-smeared video screen before there was a change in engine tone and the announcement that they were descending into Hanoi.

Noi Bai airport was a vast chaos of cavernous ceilings and endless swarming spaces that made Adelaide airport seem serene. Leon strode behind the coughing woman because she looked like she knew where to go, and after a long hike they latched onto an exhausted queue.

Somehow they'd chosen the slowest line and it took an aeon and scornful glares by the green-uniformed customs man before he was through and able to collect his case. He towed it hurriedly towards where a group of people, some holding up signs with names, were waiting for disembarking passengers. Leon's eyes ached as he searched for Alena's lovely face and blonde hair.

As the crowd dissipated, he was approached by a huge Asian bloke holding a sign scrawled with the words 'Mister Leon Shulz'.

'Mr Schuz?'

Leon nodded. 'Schulz? Yes? Where's Alena…?'

'No worry, sir. Arena send me get you. Photo shoot in Harong Bay cancel. Bad weather. She hae to go.'

'Go?'

'To Miran, sir. In Itary. Photo shoot there now on a rake. Magazine change rocation. She sorry. Come. We go hotel. Tomorrow you fry Itary.'

'What? I don't want to go to bloody Italy. I want Alena here. Like we planned. Who the hell…'

'Sir, no worry. Come. Very nie fligh tomorrow. Busneth crath. Very nie for rich people rike you, heh heh…'

Leon glared at the man. He was tall with rugby player shoulders and a strainer-post neck. He was wearing a crisp white shirt and expensive-looking tan trousers.

Outside the terminal, a pack surged. Tourists were being besieged by a gauntlet of taxi drivers.

'You know the hotel I'm going to?' Leon asked.

'Sure. Sky Pagoda. Hau Long Stree. Very nie prae.' The man grabbed the handle of Leon's case and before Leon could protest began towing it through the grubby glass doors.

'Wait…' Leon called but the man strode straight into the crowd like a battleship amongst a fleet of dinghies. Leon followed, sucked along in the slipstream. He was led to a small grey sedan that vaguely resembled a Mazda. The rugby player opened the boot and threw in Leon's case. He then opened a rear door and steered Leon in, smiling like a serial killer who knows his victim cannot get away.

The engine fired with a clatter that sent vibrations through the thin rear seat. The car shot forward. From that moment on, the rugby player acted as if he was in a formula one race. They screamed out of the car park and into a crowded road which led into an even more congested multi-lane thoroughfare. Motorbikes weaved past Leon's window so close he could see individual hairs on the riders' arms. A billboard of a beautiful Asian woman with European facial features and unbelievably white teeth holding up a giant tube of toothpaste briefly filled his view.

He leant his head back and closed his aching eyes, trying to shut out this crazy world he'd flown into. He turned his mind to Alena.

The impossible vision of her had appeared as if sent by God in the evening stillness of the farmhouse. That was almost a year ago. He'd been monitoring wheat prices when her face appeared in a pop-up ad at the side of his laptop screen. The delicious surprise of that moment would be with him forever, no matter what happened now. For looking out at him had been the face of Alice. Generous, kind Alice who didn't care about money or possessions, but people – the little kids she taught in the local school, her friends and family. Him. Their daughter who was stillborn at twenty-eight weeks.

Even now, thirty years after cervical cancer took Alice so early in their marriage, he woke up and went to sleep thinking about her. Often she came to him in his dreams. Sometimes the two of them walking with a laughing little girl between them, swinging from their hands. Three people connected into a single entity. And when he woke to reality, to thousands of acres of loneliness, he felt a stabbing agony of emptiness that turned such days into a zombie like trance of unbearable pain.

Now he could not believe a girl who looked so like Alice existed out there, the evidence clear and real on his laptop screen. A stunning model, explained the brief descriptor, as if Alena was a new tractor. For weeks, he'd gone back and logged into the Russian Brides website, thought about that face all day as he worked on the farm, rushing inside whenever possible to check that she was still there and available. Every moment had been filled with fear that someone else would snap her up, or that he'd dreamt her. But she stayed, and so when he'd thought about it for so long that he'd talked himself into it, he made contact, his finger trembling on the Enter key as if it was a door handle to an unreal terrifying world. Since the moment he'd pressed that key, he'd been propelled, stumbling to each next step with silent terror twisting his guts, not knowing how to turn back. Not wanting to turn back.

The driver said something indistinct above the conversation of duelling horns and strident motorbikes. Leon opened his eyes as the car jerked to a halt. A smiling wrinkled hotel porter wearing a faded maroon uniform with worn threads furring the collar opened his door.

Leon got out.

The burly driver was already hulking at the car door and nodding vigorously towards the tall blue building. 'Sky Pagoda, very nie.'

'Er… Is this it?' It didn't seem as regal as in the internet photos when Alena had recommended it for the nights they would spend together in Hanoi.

Minutes later, he was being shown into his upstairs room by the porter and the driver, who acted as if he owned the place.

The room was nothing like the pictures on the internet. Leon could hear street noise through the single window. He thought of the money he'd spent on this dump – he could have bought new tyres for the ute. There were some papers on the small double bed.

The driver picked them up. 'This one ticket to Itary. Tomorrow, leben p.m. This one insurance in case prane crashing, heh heh. Sorry,' he added quickly, noticing Leon's expression. 'Prane hardry eber crash. You sreep now. Oh, and one thing more.' He leant under the bed and pulled out a small pink suitcase. 'You take this one too. It Arena's. You take it to Miran too, okay?'

Leon looked at the suitcase. It was feminine and cheap-looking. A pink plastic tag was tethered to it.

'But, you know…I can't…someone else's bag…'

The driver looked at Leon as if he was a misguided toddler and said, 'Arena, she need this case. She bring it from Russia but forget it in rush to go Itary.'

'Well, look, she can simply buy another one, or I'll buy one for her, better than this. Er…if necessary.'

The driver shook his head. 'This one special one of Arena's. Senmental for her. Berong her mother. Very important. Now, you sreep. I come back tomorrow ebening eight o'crock, take you airport.'

When the driver and porter had gone, Leon sat on the bed feeling very awake. He took out his phone and sent a text to Alena.

I'm in the Sky Pagoda Hotel. What's happening? I want to talk to you.

He went over to the window and peered out. A brick wall rimed with toxic-looking black dust was half a metre from the window. He heard raucous traffic and a burst of tinny music. He turned back to the pink suitcase. Inside, it was completely bare, though it had a satin pink lining which he was able to unzip. Where were Alena's clothes if she'd brought it from Russia? He searched every centimetre of the case, feeling and poking everywhere. Maybe there were drugs inside the frame? He had no way of knowing without drilling out the industrial-looking rivets, which were a different colour to the rest of the frame. The rectangular tubular frame itself seemed too large for the size of the case. But he was no expert, having never travelled far.

His phone beeped and he rushed over to the bed.

My lovly lion I am so sorry I will c you soon please bring the pink case to Milano.

Leon shook his head. He didn't come down in the last dust storm, as his father used to say, especially when about to part with money. He felt betrayal crushing his heart, his dreams dissolving like his laptop in shutdown. He'd found it a gut-churning wrench to spend money on this trip, and sending it by electronic transfer had nauseated him. As he'd seen his bank balance reduce with a few clicks, albeit by a relatively tiny amount for him, he'd kept thinking of the fertiliser and diesel he could have bought, the real useful things he could see and smell and that would benefit the farm. It was small consolation that he hadn't yet booked their flights back to Australia from Hanoi, thinking they would have a great honeymoon in Vietnam. He was an expert at getting his money's worth. Anger welled in him. Anger at himself, and Alena, or whatever her name was. What a dope to think such a beautiful girl would be genuinely interested in a mid-fifties farmer twenty-plus years her senior. No one could replace Alice, he'd always known it. That's why he'd stayed single all these years.

She wouldn't call. For eight months, he'd been begging her to talk to him on the phone. But she'd always come up with an excuse not to, and now he knew why. Because she didn't exist. He didn't want to believe it but it appeared he'd been conducting a relationship with some rip-off international gang, not a beautiful Russian model on a photo shoot. These bastards were so clever that maybe they had found a photo of Alice, knew somehow that he was still single and wealthy and planted that pop-up ad on a website they knew he went to often. The internet was a conduit of lies. A honey trap. A sewer populated with dream-stealers.

His phone rang.

'Lion?'

'Alena?' He felt himself reeling and sat on the bed.

'Yes, my lovely Lion.' Her voice was like honey, soft and meltingly feminine, and oh so like Alice's. She had an accent, sort of Russian, he thought.

'Oh, Ali…Alena. Your voice…I can't believe it.'

'Believe it, Lion. Look. I tell you what appen. The magazine. They want me in Milano. The weather, you see. It raining in Halong Bay, so they have to change venue, take whole crew to Italy. The sun is shining here, they want photo shoot at Lake Como. It is beautiful, Lion. Please you come. Your ticket it is there, no?'

'But, er…'

'It business class. Very nice. I make the company buy ticket for you so you can come because they make me let you down in Hanoi. And you will bring my pink suitcase for me, won't you, my honey?'

'Well, all right, I s'pose. But this suitcase – it's your mother's?'

'Yes. Definitely. You must bring. Put some of your clothes in it.'

'But why this particular one? I'll buy you another one, even better.'

'That is kind but no, this one it is a precious gift from my mother in St Petersburg. Very sentimental. My lovely Lion. We will soon be together on your farm in Australia. No need to worry about anything. I already feel your hands on my body. Mmm.'

Leon paced the cramped room. He too felt his hands on her body, and her hands on his. He could post the case directly to the farm in Australia, but then if it had drugs in it, he could still be in the poo big time.

He said, 'I've got an idea. In the morning I'll wrap it up and post it directly to your hotel in Milan? We can pick it up from there.'

The reply was a rustling static, like heavy rain or someone eating dry cereal.

'Alena?'

'I sorry. I must have case straight away. For my clothes and everything. The company and my friends giving us many things for our marriage, our new life together. I want to bring them to your farm. Need suitcase. If you post, it might be lost somewhere.'

'Okay, so I'll buy you a new one in Milan, or here in Hanoi.'

There was a long pause. Strange voices, grunts. Her sweet voice came back trembling now. 'Lion, I always travel with that one. My mother's suitcase brings me luck. I am lost without it. I can't have a nice honeymoon without my precious case that my mother gave me. Please understand, my love. Please say you will bring it and I will meet you at the hotel in Milano.'

'I'm worried. You didn't meet me here in Hanoi, Alena. I am very upset, angry. Because you promised.'

'I know, Lion, I so sorry. The company fly me to Vietnam from Russia like we planned, but weather change so we must now meet in Italy.'

There was a sob in her voice and Leon felt the cracks of doubt in his heart healing.

'My friend, he picks you up, no? And I have business class ticket for you, no? To meet me here? Please, Lion. In a few days, I finish the shoot on Lake Como then we will be together. I want you inside me. Mmm. Oh, cannot wait.'

Leon looked at the business class air ticket on the bed, heard the quarrel of beeping horns in the outside night. He wanted to leave this crowded noisy country as soon as possible. The plane ticket would let him do that. He wondered how much it cost. He shouldn't waste it. Transport to the airport was already arranged and would cost him nothing. And what if Alena was real? He deserved this one chance to replace Alice, didn't he? If she wasn't real, he'd get the police onto these arseholes, then have a look around Milan and get a flight home. He had a whole day tomorrow to sort out the pink case, pry open the handle and check for drugs or find an identical one and substitute it.

'All right. I'll come.'

'I love you, my honey.'

'I love you too.'

'And the case, Lion? You bring it?'

'I'll bring it.'

After they hung up, a wave of homesickness enveloped him. The international clock on his mobile told him it was 11.14 p.m. on the farm.

When daylight smudged through the pathetic window, Leon woke, surprised at how rested he felt. Maybe the ascetic bed had done him good. After a surprisingly tasty breakfast downstairs, he stepped out into Hau Long Street. The sea of movement and chaotic noise initially shocked him and he had to stop for a moment to regather his composure. A few metres from the hotel doorway sat an old woman surrounded by plastic wrapped packets of cigarettes and dusty cans of drinks. She caught Leon staring and smiled warmly at him. Poor old lady, he thought. The thought of being poor terrified him.

Across the street, over the heads of zipping scooters and suicidal cyclists, he saw a narrow shop doorway crowded with cases and backpacks. Just what I need, he thought. He stepped off the footpath, tried to dodge a scooter that suddenly appeared and found that he'd stepped into the path of another one, then another. He retreated.

A bent-over bloke wearing what appeared to be black pyjamas

strode directly into the maelstrom of buzzing machines. Instead of being hit as Leon felt sure he would, the man walked at an even pace in a straight line and the traffic went around him as if he were a moving island. Another man, young and confident-looking, stepped off the footpath and Leon latched on like a pilot fish and followed him through the traffic. Soon he was on the other side.

He looked at the travel cases stacked around the doorway of the shop. They left just enough room to get through and once he was inside, the place was so piled with cases, packs, backpacks, wallets, handbags and purses that he could barely move.

'Your lucky morning, sir.' A teenage girl in a red sweat top and acid-wash jeans that had overdosed on the acid appeared. 'You like? Which colour? Good price today. It my birthday. Your lucky day, sir.' Her round face was smooth and smiling, her chocolate eyes bright and friendly.

'I, er…a pink suitcase.'

'Your lucky day, sir. We have many. You buy two, one for wife? Some little ones for grandchildren?'

'No, I want just a particular pink one. Pink. You got any pink ones, please?'

'Your lucky day. I have many.' She clutched his forearm and dragged him stumbling through a narrow gap. She pointed to a case the exact pink shade as the one in his hotel room. It would have been perfect had it not been the size of a small car.

'This one very good quality. Nie colour.'

'No. Sorry. It's too big. You got a smaller one, this exact colour?'

She grabbed his wrist and towed him further into the labyrinth. She pointed at a cluster of cases that were the approximate size of Alena's, but unfortunately none were pink.

'These you like. Perfec size. How many you want? Special price for my birthday.'

'The size of this one is right.' With a finger, he reached up and tapped a brown case that was hanging from the ceiling. 'But it must be pink, like that other one.'

'Oh.' The girl looked crestfallen for a nanosecond and then burst into another sales pitch. 'You buy this one brown, and then also the big pink one. Have one of each. Perfec.'

Leon felt the cases closing in on him. He had to get out of the claustrophobic shop. This silly girl was never going to talk him into spending money on something not exactly right.

'I'm sorry. I'll think about it, and come back later.'

She looked at him mournfully. 'But by then the birthday sale be over. You buy now, get discount. No discount later.'

You should be in school, he felt like saying. Where were her parents? Why didn't these people get their act together? He heard a tubercular cough from somewhere in the rear darkness of the shop.

Talking constantly, she followed him as he tried to escape, praising his good looks, his wisdom, his beautiful eyes.

He walked away feeling terrible and headed up the street. Her earnest pressuring had annoyed him, but unlike his contempt for salespeople in Australia, he felt a bit sorry for her. He walked past overstocked little shops, hurrying young people, ambling old people, women sitting on the footpath or on their haunches selling everything that they could fit in their little arena of allotted space. A couple with Australian accents were arguing with one of them. Leon was shocked by the contrast: their pastel Nike T-shirts and designer jeans and the brown formless clothing of the squatting old woman; strident wealth meets poverty's steady upward gaze. He caught some of the conversation and worked out the tourists were quibbling over something less than ten Australian cents.

A little further on, he watched a thin boy wearing only a pair of filthy shorts rifling meticulously through a rubbish bin; and an ancient man bowed under the weight of huge bowls of vegetables suspended from a wooden pole across bony shoulders. He saw a money exchange kiosk and handed over a hundred Australian dollars. The pile of Vietnamese dong he received was so unexpectedly big that he feared it wouldn't fit in his pockets. He turned back towards the hotel.

The old woman at the door of the Sky Pagoda smiled and gave him a leathery wave. He stopped and looked at the cans she was selling. He touched a can of beer with a fingertip and raised an eyebrow at her. She said a number. A quick calculation in his head told him a can was about fifty Australian cents. She looked at him with big brown eyes, her face crinkled in the warmest smile Leon had ever seen, and nodded. The old woman clearly had not been to the same school of hard sell retail as the luggage girl. He glanced across the street at the shop. The girl was sitting on a stool at the front reading a huge book and taking notes with a pencil. He watched her for a while and did not see one person go into her overstocked shop.

He turned away from the old woman and walked boldly into the teeming traffic.

The girl spotted him coming and switched on a glowing smile. 'You buy luggage now?'

'What are you reading?' he asked, looking at the book now sitting on the stool. It was a thick tome covered in Vietnamese words.

'Oh?' It took her a moment to realise what he was asking. 'Studying. You want to buy a luggage?'

'What are you studying? School?'

'Oh? I want to be accountant, also one day open more shop.'

'How old are you?'

'Fifteen. I like to work hard and study. Cannot go to school. Have to run shop. I sorry.'

'Oh no, it's okay. Is your family helping you?'

'Yes. My mother and father, they start this shop. Now my mother died, my father he help but he sick now.'

'Look. I'm only after one particular case and you don't have it. How much would you sell me that big pink case for?'

She said a price and Leon almost gasped at how cheap it was — not much more than twenty Australian dollars. He pulled out a wad of Vietnamese dong, counted out the asking price. As he was about to give it to her, he stopped, added another handful of notes forcing himself not to look at the denominations.

For once, she seemed momentarily speechless as she looked at the stack of notes. 'I not sleep with you.'

'What? No. Look. You…it's your birthday.'

'I get you the case.'

'No. I don't want it. I just want you to have this money. Help you with your study. Something real.'

'Where you from?'

'Australia.'

'Australia. Kangaroo. Thank you.'

Back across the street, he stopped by the smiling old lady. She appeared not to have sold a single can of anything since he inspected her supply when he'd first emerged from the hotel. He didn't normally drink – he baulked at the prices in Australia and stuck to plain rainwater – but now looking for an excuse to give her money, he picked two cans of beer and she fished out a wrinkled plastic bag and put them in it. He added it up to be about thirty dong but he peeled off a hundred and put it in her outstretched hand.

She stared down at it for a moment and then looked up at him.

'I'm s'posed to haggle, I know,' he said. 'But I've got all this strange money and you…' Her grin got wider and she nodded at him, secreting the notes somewhere in her thin clothing. She plopped an extra can in the plastic bag, reached up a hand and touched his.

A sense of peace came over him that he hadn't felt since before Alice died. 'Thanks,' he said.

She smiled in reply.

In the hotel room, Leon stuffed the beers in the fridge's tiny freezer compartment and cranked up the dial to maximum cold. Then he lay on the bed flicking through television channels with the remote. The air conditioner shuddered on the wall but thankfully shot out an icy typhoon. The internet descriptor of the hotel had said he would have a huge range of English-speaking pay TV channels but he could only find Vietnamese programs.

He kept looking over at the pink suitcase. He got up. Shaking and turning it gave him no clues. The incongruous rivets were solid and he sat on the bed and picked at the fat metal frame trying to find an opening so that he could inspect the inside of the square tubing. He sniffed and shook and prodded at every section of the case. He tried to guess its weight by lifting it with each arm, wondering if he was imagining that it seemed heavy for its size.

After a while, he gave up and fished a beer from the freezer. The top of the can was frosted with dust and he washed all the cans with water from the skinny plastic bottles in the bathroom. The water bottle labels read optimistically 'Joyful to Everyone'. The first beer went down quickly and he clacked open another. He lay on the bed and picked up the remote.

He found a Vietnamese game show, a kind of *Price Is Right*. The prizes astonished him – a garden hose, some toothpaste same as he'd seen on the billboard near the airport, a wheelbarrow. He thought of the booming price of wheat and a boy searching through rubbish; rich tourists haggling over a few cents as if it was a game they had to win; a teenage girl studying on the footpath in case she missed a customer; the serene solitude of his farm and this crowded spaceless country; the healthy sums in his farm accounts which even as he watched them grow were never enough; the reality of his memories of Alice versus a mirage on a laptop screen. I've betrayed you, Alice, and I don't know what to do, a voice cried in his head, and a jolt of searing heartache overwhelmed him. This often happened and he steeled himself for the pain. Then another voice came. Alice. Yes, you do, my Lion. You know what to do.

He sat up so quickly beer sloshed out of the can's mouth. He got his smart phone out and logged into the hotel's wi-fi.

Afterwards, he went downstairs. The street seemed marginally quieter now in the damp heat of early afternoon. He weaved through crowds, sweat already sticking his shirt to his body. It took a while but he eventually found what he was looking for. He completed his business and went back to the hotel. He sipped at the last can of beer, the old lady's gift, while he got ready.

Tears leaked onto his cheeks as he did so. Perhaps it was the unfamiliar alcohol making him emotional. But he knew it was something far deeper in his soul than that. This whole experience had brought back vividly those memories of what he called his last of happiness. That too brief time married to Alice.

Occasionally he found himself like this – crying – alone, working, in the middle of the day, anytime. It could be a seeing a newborn lamb, a rainbow, the trees they planted together now a forest, the kangaroo that Alice called Rag Ear who came each summer evening to graze on the front lawn, the new play areas at the primary school that came from his yearly anonymous donation. Things that should bring joy but hadn't done so for decades. In those moments, a moan of grief would start deep in his soul and emerge as a child-like cry. He'd let it all come and wait for the softening. Somehow the tears and the cry helped.

At five o'clock, he checked that the hotel lobby was deserted before he strode quickly through it towing his suitcase. As he passed the beer lady and her dusty cans, he handed her an envelope he'd taken from the hotel room. It was fat with dong. He couldn't meet her eyes – he didn't feel generous. But he was glad that his parents were long dead and couldn't see him giving money away.

Soon he was sitting on a stool inside the suitcase shop while the girl hailed a taxi for him. Before he went out to the waiting driver, he handed her an envelope even fatter than the one he'd given the old lady. 'Happy birthday. Don't open it till I'm gone. I hope you won't be insulted – it's just that… I dunno.'

'It not my birthday.' She stared at her feet.

'That's okay.'

'Sometimes I have to say thing to survive. I sorry.'

'I want you to write your name and address on this piece of paper. I may send you something from time to time. If that's okay?'

'Why you do this?'

'My wife.'

'She is kind person. Good person.'

'Yes. She is.'

'Yes. You too.'

In the taxi to Noi Bai, Leon checked his cheap smart phone. There were no messages.

He was pleased he'd got his money's worth from the hotel's excellent free wi-fi. Farmers are weather junkies and he'd checked the conditions at Lake Como and Halong Bay before completing his other business. According to the weather site, heavy rain and storms would still be lashing all of northern Italy, while Halong Bay was sunny. He noted the time before pocketing the phone. The driver would be looking for him at the Sky Pagoda at about the time he would be squeezing into his seat for the flight home to his part of this lopsided world. Economy class.